ENTICED BY A STREET GOD

YASAUNI MCWILLIAMS

Enticed by A Street God

Published by Mz. Lady P Presents

Acknowledgments

First, I want to thank God because without him I don't know where I would be. I would like to thank my mother, Debra. She has truly been a real trooper with me, and when I'm too tired to run back and forth for her, she's understanding about it sometimes, lol.

Mz. Lady P. (Suge), you're a great publisher and thank you for not dropping me when I work your nerves, and thanks for not dropping me when I quit writing and quit the company etc., lmao. I quit a lot, and you never give up on me. You always there when I need you and I appreciate it for real.

I have to thank my Auntie Bilhah. She and my mom are the biggest fans and best supporters.

To the dream team that makes up Mz. Lady P Presents, I love y'all.

To my friend Tina, man you have become more like a sister. A lot of people have gone left on me, or we just don't talk to me because of my crazy work schedule, but you keep up with me around my schedule. You are always sound reasoning in my life and with my books. I love you.

I can't forget the best test readers in the world, Lakeitha Chatman and Shaniece McWilliams.

I know I'm probably missing a lot of people but never charge it to my heart. I love all y'all. To my readers, I give y'all a huge thank you!

Connect With Me

Instagram: Sauni
Twitter: Yasauni McWilliams@sauniD

Facebook: Yasauni Mc

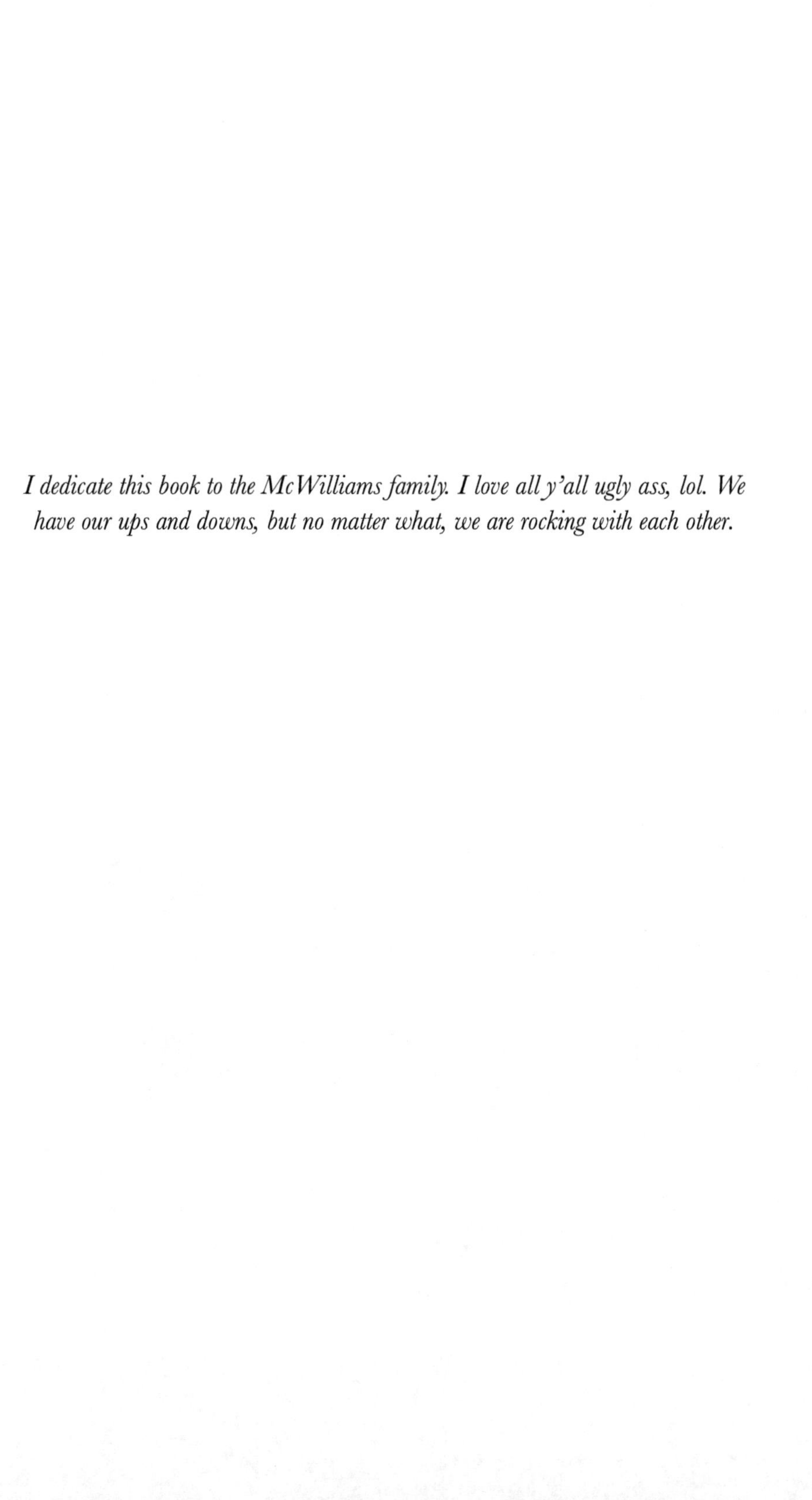

I dedicate this book to the McWilliams family. I love all y'all ugly ass, lol. We have our ups and downs, but no matter what, we are rocking with each other.

ONE

Synopsis

Crimson Anderson, the daughter of a prominent preacher, lived for doing the right thing and following her father's rules to the letter. Not wanting to cause backlash or unwanted attention, she happily played her part as the sweet and dutiful daughter standing by her father's side. One night of an inevitable mishap and meeting what she considered a "common thug" drastically change her view on what she considered a happy life.

After his brother's reign of terror, Quinton decided that running the streets with respect more so than fear would keep him from an untimely and brutal demise. Having everything he could have wanted in life and any woman he wanted when his time permitted, he was more than baffled running into a woman that would make him reconsider his lifestyle.

Relationships will form, loyalty will be tested, and betrayal comes from every angle. In this twist of fate, how will Crimson adjust to being Enticed by a Street God?

TWO

Crimson Anderson

I stood in the parking lot next to my bestie looking under the hood of the car as if we knew what we were doing. The car had stopped in the middle of the street. Thank God that there are still some decent men in the world. They pushed it into a parking lot for us. I was grateful for that, but we still had a problem, we were stranded. Since we were kids Keyionte' has always gotten us into some type of jam. Being the daughters of a minister and a pastor, we were always supposed to be on our best behavior. You know how it is. We had to walk, talk, and breathe the way that the church expected us to. I, for one, was about sticking to the rules. I never wanted to embarrass my father. We had an entire congregation watching. I'm usually on my best behavior, until we add Keyionte' into the mix.

She was the best friend I could ever have, but she was the reason for all my punishments. My best friend was the type that made all the things they say about church girls true, but I wouldn't have her any other way. I watched her as she messed with some wires on the car, and it started smoking out of nowhere. We both jumped back.

"Jesus Keyionte'. What did you do?" My heart was pounding.

She was trying to take us out. She laughed at me, but I kept moving backward just in case the car caught fire.

"Girl, you know your dad wouldn't approve of you using Jesus in that sentence." She was right, but if he'd seen Keyionte' make smoke appear out of thin air, he would've said worst.

"We need to just call my dad and have him pick us up." I pulled out my iPhone holding it in front of my face to unlock it.

"Yeah, that's a good idea," she retorted, rolling her eyes.

"Then how are we supposed to get home?" I asked still holding my phone out with my finger hovering over my dad's number.

"We'll figure that out along the way, but I don't feel like explaining to our fathers why we are in Humboldt Park. Do you?" she asked me seriously.

I wasn't into lying to my dad. I didn't just offer up information neither. The truth was I would rather walk to the south suburbs than to tell him where we are. I stared down at the riding boots on my feet that came up to my thighs. It was chilly out here, and I knew once the sun went down, it was going to be downright cold. Winters in Chicago were brutal. I had on fleece leggings under my calf-length skirt, but that wouldn't keep me warm for too long. I knew we should've taken my car, but having an overprotective dad meant having a locator on my car. We only came out here to go shopping, and even with us being twenty years old, our dads didn't approve. As long as we were under their roofs, we had to abide by their rules and moving out wasn't an option until marriage. Yeah, our dads were as old school as ever.

"We can catch an Uber. I have the app." I rolled my eyes at her.

"That doesn't surprise me," I responded with my eyebrow arched at her as a white and chrome Range Rover with tinted windows pulled into the parking lot.

It seemed like both doors opened simultaneously, and a black Air Jordan hit the pavement from the driver's side of the truck. He stepped back closing the door, and my body went into an overdrive of lust-filled emotions. He had on an all-black Balmain hoodie with matching black jeans. His skin was smooth and the color of dark chocolate. He had jet black hair with a fresh cut, and his lining was crisp. He smiled at us, and my knees got weak.

"You ladies need some help?" the driver spoke walking up to us.

I was so entranced by his looks and demeanor that I hadn't paid attention to the passenger walking up to Keyionte'. My eyes roamed over the common thug that was commanding my attention as I cleared my throat.

"No, we're good, thank you," I replied quickly, only to be interrupted by the passenger.

"It doesn't look like y'all good. It looks like this motherfucker needs to be in the junkyard," he stated, frowning at the smoking car.

I rolled my eyes at his rude comment. I had told Keyionte' the same thing plenty of times, but we didn't know this man, so who was he to give us his unwanted opinion. My eyes searched over him taking in his outfit. He had on a pair of white and red Jordan's with some ripped white jeans, and a Pelle with rhinestones and studs all over it. He had to be about six feet three inches because he towered over her small frame. His locks were freshly twisted hanging down his back, and his light brown skin was smooth and youthful. He almost looked innocent, but it was something about his eyes that didn't sit right with me. I cocked my head to the side. Looking at him, he was your typical flashy thug, and I could tell that he was bad news. He was just the type of man that Keyionte' was drawn to, and the type that I stayed away from at all cost.

"My name is Quinton." The driver held his hand out toward me to shake mine.

When I gave my hand to him, he grabbed my fingers giving them a gentle squeeze. Although his hands were almost as soft as mine were, his index finger was rough with a callous. *That is weird* I thought to myself before dropping my hand from his. He took a step back after assessing my expression. I'm pretty sure my face was telling him that I didn't want to be bothered, although my body was sending signals to step closer and wrap myself around this man.

"I'm Crimson, and that's my friend Keyionte'." I pointed to her and noticed she was all in his friend's face. I rolled my eyes for the second time within two minutes.

"I forgot about the rude nigga to my right. That's Martell." Quinton stated with a smirk on his face.

"Nigga, I know you didn't give that girl my government? You can call me Rush," he retorted with a mug on his face.

I was a good judge of character, and that was fitting for him, he seemed like the type that sped through life without learning a thing.

"Let me see what I can do for you ladies."

Quinton walked to the car looking under the hood. I could tell from the way that he was toying with whatever he wasn't the type to fix cars. He was too put together, his hands were too soft, not one chipped nail, he was too clean. Although he came off nice to me, I could tell he wasn't the type of man that people played with. Suddenly a spark shot from the car while he was messing with something. He jumped back looking around.

"Girl, what the fuck have you done to this car?" He turned looking at me, but I pointed to Keyionte' as Rush laughed shaking his head, giving us an 'I told you so' expression that I wanted to wipe off his face.

"Look, hop in my truck, and I'll take you two where you need to go," Quinton told us. Keyionte' started pulling our shopping bags out of the car, and Rush helped her to transfer them into the Range.

"What the heck are you doing, Keyionte'? We don't know them and you ready to hope in their truck because it's expensive. This is how women come up missing." I crossed my arms over my chest. She couldn't be this stupid or this hard up for a man. She stopped putting our bags in the Range and walked over to me.

"Crimson, if we have them to take us home, I can save a lot of money. Seeing that we just went crazy tearing the mall down, I would like to keep some of that in my pocket."

This girl killed me acting as if she was hard up for money. We both made a decent amount of money working for the church. Not to mention, our fathers wasn't hurting in the money department. A cab ride home wouldn't put a dent in either of our accounts and that's after dropping about two grand a piece at the mall.

"I will replace the money you spend on us getting home," I stated seriously. I again thought about how I should have driven my own car to the mall, but Keyionte' insisted on driving. My dad always said to follow my first mind because it's usually the right one.

"Why spend any of our money if we don't have to. Plus, I want to get to know Rush better, and a ride to Country Club Hills from here will let me feel him out a little more."

Just as I expected it was all about the man. Don't get me wrong. Rush was a fine specimen, but his demeanor and attitude said he was nothing but trouble.

"I'll catch a cab," I told her. I had to find the main street and pray a yellow cab rode down it.

I began to walk away, with my phone in my hand googling for a yellow cab. I knew nothing about this part of Chicago, but it couldn't be that bad with all these white people walking their dogs.

"Yo, wait up." I turned to see Quinton running up to me. I stopped watching the Range Rover pull off into traffic.

"What are you doing here?" I asked looking at the back of the truck he was driving not too long ago.

"You weren't comfortable riding in the car with us, and it was obvious your friend is feeling my nigga Rush. Instead of leaving you by yourself, I told her that I would go with you." He smiled at me, and my heart did a double beat.

"Thank you, but I'm good."

I began to walk away from him. As much as he was being a gentleman, it didn't change the fact that I didn't know him. He grabbed me by my arms turning me to him.

"Check it out. I'm not a man that's used to the word no, and this is the second time you have turned your back on me today. If this relationship is going to work between us, we have to get a few things out of the way."

I stood there stunned. Again, I didn't know this man, and he was reprimanding me without raising his voice. However, the tone of his voice was what really made me give him my undivided attention. What did he mean if this relationship was going to work? I haven't even agreed to let him ride with me home.

"I understand that you are used to getting your way, but like I said I'm fine." My voice went up a couple of octaves.

I didn't even know why I was acting like this with him. I knew he wouldn't hurt me. His vibes are the complete opposite of his friends. I thought about Keyionte', and I shouldn't have let her leave with Rush.

"We can do this your way or my way. We can get in a cab of your choosing, or we can get in this car I had my brother to bring to me. The choice of how we get you home is yours, but me going with you is your only option."

I smiled shaking my head pointing to the Mercedes Benz that was identical to mine. Quinton nodded his head, and the person driving the car pulled up to us getting out of the car.

"Yo, G?" The guy gave us a chin tip.

"Major, this is your sister-in-law Crimson, and Crimson this is our brother Major," Quinton said it so casually that I almost believed him.

"What up, sis?" Major said, getting into a black Benz truck before I could respond.

"Come on, ma. It's cold out here."

I got in the car, and Quinton made sure that I was completely in before he closed the door for me. I leaned over pulling the handle and pushing the door out a little for him.

"I see you have manners."

I smiled at him. He was surprised to find that out about me, but it was really me that was surprised by him. Any other man would have left me standing on the corner just as my best friend did. Even though I felt like he wouldn't sale me off into human trafficking, once I put my seatbelt on, I leaned on the door away from him.

THREE

Quinton

Crimson had run her address down to me, and I knew exactly where she lived, I was in that part of town all the time, and I hadn't seen her around. If I had, I would've remembered. This girl was pretty as hell with natural red hair. When she told me her name was Crimson, I knew right off why her parents named her that. Her crimson colored hair accented her toasted brown skin tone and brown eyes. She is about five feet seven inches, and even though her clothes weren't form fitting, I could tell that she had a nice shape to her. I didn't know anything about this girl, but for the first time in my life, I wanted to know everything about a woman. Being in my profession, I didn't believe in getting close to people. They let you down when shit gets hard. I took my eyes off the road and glanced at her.

"Tell me about yourself, ma."

I watched her as she folded her hands in her lap, and then crossed her legs at the ankle. I could tell someone had put her through etiquette classes at some point and time in her life. I smiled a little because I could tell that she was nervous, and that was the last thing I wanted her to be around me. She cleared her throat.

"What do you want to know?" she asked me in a voice above a whisper.

To have a woman feeling shy around me was so uncommon these days. I usually have women flocking to me trying to throw the pussy at me from all angles, so her bashfulness was refreshing.

"Anything you want to tell me," I responded to her cutting my eyes at her again.

She pursed her lips and then bit down on her bottom lip, causing a dimple to wink at me. My dick jumped at her motions. In this the moment, I knew that I would do anything to get Crimson and keep her. I already knew she was different from what I was used to, so I would have to step outside my box for her.

"I'm in school for communications and religious studies, my dad is a pastor, and I love God."

I nodded my head. We had something in common. I loved God too. I wonder what she would say if I told her when my brother called me G, that was an acronym for God. I smiled not realizing that she was watching me.

"Why the sinister smile?" I filtered the smile on my face giving her a genuine one.

"Nothing really, it's just the way you said you love God." She frowned a little, and her dimple came out again.

"Is something funny about that?" Her tone changed, and she was ready to challenge me. I wanted to see what would happen.

"Yes," I baited her.

She gave me a quizzical expression, and I wondered if she would go all church girl on me, or if she would get all mad like most people that felt they had to prove a point about God. I was aware that I was walking a tight rope, especially when it came to religion. People would show their true colors. Religious people did everything that the bible said not to do. I'm not saying that I don't believe in God because I do, I just wanted to see how she would act. Was she one of those people that felt like if you didn't believe what they did, she would spite me down?

"I don't like to play games with people Quinton, and you are trying to get a rise out of me. It's not going to work."

Damn, she called me on my bullshit. People never did that to me. Why would they? No one ever questioned God.

I pulled up to her house, and she opened the door getting out of the car as if the seat was on fire.

"Yo, wait up." She stopped in the middle of the sidewalk looking around like she was expecting someone to pop up out of nowhere. "You didn't even thank me for the ride with your ungrateful ass." She cocked her head at me.

"Thank you!" The words were on her lips as I snatched her phone from her hand putting my number in it. I made sure to call my phone. Once I heard my phone ring over the speakers, I hung up, handing it back to her.

"I may seem ungrateful, but you're rude," she said before walking away.

"Call me tomorrow!" I yelled at her retreating back as she disappeared behind the door.

"I can't believe this shit," I said aloud to myself walking to my car. Crimson had turned her back to me again, and if she wanted to play these games, then I would play them with her.

FOUR

Keyionte'

"What's up with some of that pussy?" As I eyeballed the nigga sitting next to me, I would say I was appalled, but I knew the makings of a thug, and I loved them.

Yeah, I was what people considered a church girl. I was there every time the doors opened unless I was at school. My parents weren't having that girl's gone wild shit with me, but what they didn't know wouldn't hurt them. The more they threw in my face that I needed to be more like Crimson, the wilder I got. Don't get me wrong. I loved my friend. She was more like a sister to me, but she was lame. She wasn't willing to have her father looking down on her. She did everything he told her to and walked the straight and narrow.

"I'm not about to give you none of this. We just met fifteen minutes ago." I used my hand motioning down to my honey pot, and he smirked at me.

"I thought they said church girls were freaks?" he retorted.

Messing with thug ass niggas was engraved into my soul. I knew that they were the ones for me out of all types of men in the world. I checked out Rush's brown skin, dreads that hung down his back, and his thick frame. Damn, he was one of the finest niggas I've come up on in a minute. From the way he and his friend were dressed, I knew they had to be into some shit heavy as hell, so it was only right that I played wifey or side bitch for a while.

"Just because I'm a freak doesn't mean that I'm fucking you tonight or any other night for that matter." I looked him in his eyes as I told him that.

"Stop playing with me, bruh. You knew as soon as you saw me that we were going to fuck. I figure we take out all that extra shit and get down to it."

He was dead ass serious, and I wasn't sure if I should be offended or respect how he came off. Before I could respond, he had pulled his dick out of his pants. Most females would be turned off or scared that they were about to get raped, but it had my panties so wet it was crazy. I licked my lips at the thought of trying to fit his entire dick in my mouth. I felt like he challenged me when he pulled that monster out of his pants.

I swallowed the Mentos that I had in my mouth and leaned my head over in his lap. He took in a deep breath at the cool but warm sensation that came over the mushroomed head. I inched my mouth down over him. It was so fat that it was stretching my jaws, and I didn't even have half of him in my mouth.

This is the part where people would call me a hoe for sucking this man's dick down the street from my house after knowing him for less than an hour. Personally, I don't give a damn what people say because I do what I want when I want, and what I wanted right now was to make this man's dick disappear. When I finished polishing him off, I opened the door and spat out his kids.

"You did all of that and about to leave my kids out in the cold. You're a disrespectful ass woman." I laughed, this man he is a nut.

We exchanged numbers, and I got out of the truck walking to my house. The last thing I needed was for my nosy snitching ass mama to see me getting out of it. I had made plans with Rush to get Crimson and my bags tomorrow. I took a deep breath before opening the door. It was time for me to pull all the theatrics out my ass. I blinked my eyes several times and then pinched my cheeks and nose to give them a little blush. As soon as tears filled my eyes, I was ready.

"Mom, dad, where are you?" I ran into the house hysterical with tears running down my face. I searched through the house finding them in the sitting room. I walked over to my mother dropping to my knees in front of her putting my head in her lap.

"What's wrong, baby?" my mother asked. Once my dad realized that I was crying, he jumped up from his favorite chair racing to us.

"I…wa-was… carjacked," I finally got the words out between sobs.

"When? Where? Are you hurt?" My mom rubbed her hands over my body looking for signs that I had been hurt. The tears were still rolling down my face.

"The car started jerking, so I stopped right outside of town hoping that if it sat for a minute the jerking would stop. Three guys walked up, snatched me out of the car, got in, and pulled off. I'm so sorry, daddy," I whimpered out the apology.

"There's nothing to be sorry for. Let's call the police, and we will go get you a new car tomorrow," my dad told me as my mother rubbed my back trying to soothe me. *Jackpot!*

In my head, I was twerking on top of our dining room table. A bitch like me deserved that new car and a Grammy for this performance. I sat there hiccupping and dry heaving until the police left. I told them three white men in black hoodies robbed me.

I went to my room, locked the door, and called Crimson while I ran myself a bath. Lying was exhausting. Crimson answered on the second ring.

"Girl, that nigga's got a big dick," was the first thing I told her when she picked up.

"Please don't tell me you had sex with him already?"

I sucked my teeth and rolled my eyes. At times, she acted like my mother instead of my friend. She acted like the Virgin Mary herself, but we both knew that wasn't the case.

"No, I gave him some head." She let out a breath.

"So, you let him have sex with your mouth instead?" I stripped out of my clothes and sat down in the steaming hot bath water.

"You're too uptight. Maybe if you let someone knock the five years of cobwebs out of your pussy, you wouldn't act this way." I imagined her pursing her lips and both of her dimples appearing in her cheeks giving her a childlike appearance.

"I see you're having a bad night. We can talk tomorrow," she said before disconnecting the call.

This wasn't the first time our calls ended like this, and it wouldn't be the last time. From the outside looking in, you would think we are frenemies, but Crimson was my bitch. I wanted nothing but the best for her, and she felt the same about me. I knew that us wanting the best for each other was totally two different things. I wanted her to see things from my point of view and vice versa. I may not have been doing things the way she wanted, but if she stepped out from under her father's wing just one time, maybe she would find herself. As of right now, she wouldn't know what she wanted if it smacked her in the face. I may not do things the way she thought I should, but right now, I'm happy with who I am.

Three Days Later

I stepped out of my black on black BMW that my dad had just coped me in front of the beauty shop where Rush told me to meet him at. I opened the door looking around, but he wasn't here.

"How can I help you?" a lady about my age asked me.

She would've been very pretty except for that huge black eye she was sporting that covered the right side of her face. She had jumped in the wrong person's face, and they had laced her ass up like a fresh frontal install.

"I'm looking for Rush. He told me to meet him here." She looked me up and down rolling her eyes.

"So you the bitch he's been fucking with?" I curled my lip at her. The last thing I had time for was an angry female that ran up on the wrong bitch and got past beat the fuck up.

"I'm not exactly sure what bitch he's been fucking, but I can assure you it's not me…yet."

I wasn't into lying to people if I couldn't benefit from it, and it was nothing that she could do for me. Hell, she couldn't bob and weave right to miss that right hook someone gave her. I smiled at her just as she took a step towards me. I hated fighting, but I was ready to make her left eye look identical to the right one.

"What the fuck you think you're doing? Get your stupid ass over here and finish your customer's head." The girl jumped at the sound of Rush's voice. He walked behind her grabbing her by the arm slinging her behind him.

"You're just going to disrespect and embarrass me like that? It's bad enough everyone sees the after effects of you, now you're doing shit with no regards to me."

Rush turned to look at her like he was about to beat her ass in front of everyone in the shop. Usually, I don't get into shit like this, but I needed my bags so he could beat her ass later. I walked behind him and called his name before putting my hand on his shoulder.

"Come on. Let's go for a ride so that you can cool off."

He turned to me with my bags still in his hands. His expression was full of tension. His hands were tight around the handles of the bags, his eyebrows were furrowed, and a thick vein popped out of his neck. I grabbed the bags out of one of his hands and then laced my fingers in his walking him towards the door.

"He's going to do you just like he does me!" the girl yelled behind us.

Rush gave her a look, and she swallowed hard looking down at her feet. I pulled him out the door behind me. That bitch had to be crazy if she thought I would let a nigga lay a hand on me. The only thing he will be laying is the pipe, and as big as his dick is, that shit had better be proper.

"Wait I don't feel like getting stranded. We can take my car." This nigga had jokes for real. I laughed all the way to my new baby.

"Damn you done came up." He got into the car sliding in on the soft leather.

"You did good, grasshopper." Rush said leaning his seat back.

FIVE

Crimson

My phone rung several times within an hour, Quinton had called twice and now Keyionte' was blowing me up. I was ready to throw my phone out of the window. Keyionte' knew that I was working today. Quinton had called twice a day for the last two weeks, and I still hadn't answered him. A lot came with talking to a guy like him, and I had to make sure he was going to be worth my time and the trouble. I knew I couldn't get to know him without talking to him, but I was scared of the unknown.

Keyionte' told me what had happened when she went to get our clothes, and it wasn't surprising to know those things happened with Rush. I stopped telling her a couple of days ago that Rush didn't mean her well. Once she's attracted to what's in men pants, it's all over, and evidently, he had the key to heavens gates because she was like a puppy following its master.

"What do you want Tae dang?" I yelled in through the phone using the nickname I donned her with when we were younger. I could tell she had her hand over the mouthpiece since I heard muffled talking in the background.

"Keyionte', why are you blowing my line up?" I asked again irritated with her.

"Come outside."

It was time for a break, so I hung up.

"Dad, I'm taking lunch." A few seconds went by and my dad yelled back okay. I forwarded the calls directly to his office, got my coat and walked out of the door. I walked out of the church and in front of me was the man I had been avoiding these last couple of weeks. I couldn't help the smile that eased its way across my face seeing him. Quinton was standing in front of me with a scowl on his face that made him look even finer.

"As intelligent as you are, you can't follow simple instructions, huh?" He opened the door to the Range for me to get in.

I walked to the truck not saying a word. I knew once he found me that he would have an attitude. I was happier than I thought I would be to see him though. As far as Keyionte' goes for giving him my whereabouts, I wasn't sure if I should strangle her or thank her, I would figure that out the next I lay eyes on her. He closed the door after I got in and walked to the driver side of the truck. Getting in, he stared at me for a minute before he pulled off.

Was it possible to miss someone that you only had a brief encounter with? I thought to myself as we both enjoyed the silence between us.

"Why didn't you answer the phone for me?"

I cut my eyes at Quinton, but his eyes were still on the road. He waited for me to answer him as I went over things that I could tell him in my head, but I decided on the entire truth.

"I'm not stupid, Quinton, I know what you do for money, and I had to figure out if I wanted to go against everything I had been taught to mess with a common thug. We come from two different worlds, and I wasn't sure if I could control the boundaries between the two. My life is uncomplicated, and I know what's to come if I mess with the type of man my father has always wanted me to date. With you, things are blurred and unknown. I know what type of life you lead, and you are a complication. Do I really want to deal with that?"

I could tell he was pondering what I said, so I waited to give him that time to think.

"First off, there's nothing common about this thug. You haven't given me a chance to clear the blurred vision that you have about me and the life I lead. I'm going to keep it one hundred with you. I do things that others feel are bad so that my family can eat, but not only that, I help my community in any way that I can. I make sure the kids in my neighborhood have clothes, shoes, and food. I never have my workers to accept anything from anyone's house because that will take away from their children. When old people get sick, I have my boys helping them and paying for meds and shit. Although I do what I do, I have found a way to do that shit respectfully and take care of people at the same time. There's more to me than what meets the eye, Crimson. You have your God, and to my people I am a God. Before you decide you don't want to fuck with me, let me show you the real me. I'm only asking you this one time, please don't make me abduct your ass because like I told you, I always get what I want."

My mouth was open, and my eyes were bucked. I had processed a lot of what he was saying until he said he would kidnap me. I closed my mouth then exhaled a breath.

"God gives people choices," I told him, staring at the side of his face.

"I gave you a choice— the easy way or the hard way, now you pick."

I couldn't help but laugh even though he was serious as hell. I would let him think he won this one, because the moment I saw him in front of my dad's church, I had chosen him.

"Where are we going? I only have an hour for lunch," I voiced as I stared out of the window.

"To this soul food spot, I'll have you back on time." I sat back and enjoyed the ride.

~

Quinton had ordered our food before we got there, so we picked up and left right back out heading back to the church. We sat in the lot eating when I saw my father walking out of the side door and tensed before realizing the tint on the window was so dark that he couldn't tell who was in here. I looked at my phone and noticed that I was ten minutes over my break. My father was about to hit the roof. He hated tardiness. I waited for my dad to go back inside the church before I looked at Quinton.

"Thanks for lunch, but I have to get back to work." He nodded his head as I cleaned up all the containers in the truck putting them into a bag so that I can trash it.

"I'm going to call you later," he said, leaning over brushing his lips across mine. I felt a blush creeping its way up to my cheeks as I smiled and got out of the car.

I walked into the church at an all-time high. Nothing could mess with my mood. I slipped out of my coat. Opening the coat closet, I put it in there, and when I closed the door, my dad was right behind it. I jumped putting my hand over my chest. My heart was pounding.

"Daddy, you scared me." I tried to get my breathing under control as he stood like a statue staring at me.

"Where have you been?" I stepped around him going to sit down. I had to weigh my words before I told him. He could get overbearing, and I hated it.

"I went to lunch with a friend." I pulled out my laptop, turned it on, and opened my spreadsheet as my father stared me down.

"Someone I know?" He was prying. It killed me when he acted like I was ten instead of closer to twenty-one.

"No, you don't know him," I answered without looking at him.

"Oh, it's a guy. You know you have to be careful with men today. All of them are not like me and have your best interest at heart."

This is around the time that I tuned him out. Most women my age had one or two kids by now or at least a boyfriend, but I had neither.

"I know, dad," I told him curtly. If it were up to my dad, no one would be good enough for me, but this speech was getting old and tired. Maybe Keyionte' was on to something telling me I needed to live my life for me.

"Invite him to church. I want to meet him." I almost laughed in his face at the idea of Quinton walking in here with Timberlands and a Pelle on.

"I'm still getting to know him, dad. We are not at the meet the parent's stage." I closed the lid on my laptop because as long as my dad was in here probing for information, I wouldn't get anything done.

"It's never too early for this young man to get my permission to date my daughter."

I cocked my head at my dad. This was going to be World War I between the man that raised me and the man that swears we're a couple.

"We'll see dad. Like I said, I'm still getting to know him."

My dad frowned and walked off without a word. This was not over, and we both knew it. I laughed at the thought of the man of God meeting the man they called God.

Two Months Later

After I did what Quinton told me and gave him a chance, I found out he was easy to fall for. I had been hearing good and bad things about him, but I let all of that go over my head because he was showing me nothing but good things. We did lunch twice a week and went out every weekend. He opened my eyes to everything that I was missing out on, and I was falling hard and fast for him.

As we walked down the street holding hands, Quinton had pulled me close to him. We turned the corner, and this girl coming out of the neighborhood store looked me up and down rolling her eyes at me. I didn't pay any attention to her. I just figured she was a girl that Quinton used to mess with. We walked a little further, and this time a male and female looked at me like I was stinking or something. I looked up at Quinton who seemed to be oblivious to the stares that we were getting, so I stopped in front of him.

"Why are they glaring at me like I did something to them?" I folded my arms across my chest, waiting for him to answer me.

"Shake that shit off, ma. Who the fuck cares. You're with me, not them." He pulled me into his arms, but I needed to know what was going on.

"Tell me now, Quinton," I raised my voice a little knowing he hated when I used that tone of voice with him.

He grabbed me by the arm pulling me in the direction of his truck. He was walking so fast that I had to take double steps just to keep up with him. My heart rate started increasing because I wasn't sure what was about to happen to me. Keyionte' had recently pulled something like this with Rush, and he smacked her so hard my teeth clicked together for her. Was Quinton about to beat my behind in this truck?

"You not about to hit me, are you?" I asked sounding like a baby that was about to get scold. He stopped with his eyes wide like I had lost my mind.

"I wasn't, but I should hit your ass for that stupid ass question. I'm only going to tell you this one more time. Hitting women isn't my thing. I may shoot a bitch every now and then, but since you're not a bitch, you don't have to worry about that."

He grabbed my hand but slowed his pace as we made our way to the car. He opened the door for me as usual, and once he got in the car, he took off towards downtown Chicago.

"Where are we going?" I asked. He didn't say a word until we pulled into a parking garage.

"Come on."

We took the elevator down walked a couple of blocks until I started seeing all high-end stores. We walked into Nieman Marcus, and he pulled several items off the racks handing them to me.

"Who are these for?" I questioned ready to find my inner ratchet chick and go crazy on him. He noticed my expression and pushed me towards the dressing room.

"They are for you. Now try them on." I looked at the skin-tight jeans and crop top hoodie then back at him.

"What's wrong with what I have on?"

I was ready to cry. I felt my lip quivering and had to bite down on it. We had been out together all this time, and he has never said anything about the way I dress. Now all of a sudden, he doesn't like my choice of clothing. I looked at the clothes he had shoveled in my hands to try on then glanced back up at him only to find him staring at me.

"Baby, I love the church girl look on you. It was one of the reasons I was drawn to you in the beginning, but if you don't want the people in my hood looking at you the way they do, you have to switch it up. I'm not trying to change you in any way, but if you are fucking with a nigga like me, you have to look and play the part. You can't half step. Now make your choice."

I looked at the items in my hand. *Do I really want to fit into his world?* I asked myself. Already knowing my answer, I shrugged my shoulders and walked into the changing room.

SIX

Quinton

I picked out a couple more things for Crimson as I waited for her to come out.

"Quinton."

I turned around and damn near had a heart attack. Her body was one of the best I've ever seen in my twenty-five years on earth. I damn near told her to put her skirt and shit back on and say fuck these clothes. She walked towards me, and from the look on her face, I know she saw my dick harden. I didn't give a fuck though. Her jeans fit her like a second skin. The small amount of stomach she showed was enticing and them damn heels she had on was about to get her innocent ass bent over in the dressing room. I couldn't let another man see her like this. She had me getting all jealous and ready to kill the imaginary nigga in my head for looking at her.

"Yeah ma, that's you." She turned around showing me her ass, and I was done for.

"Let me get you a coat and we're out of here."

I pulled the Balmain identical to mine off the rack. She walked alongside me so that I could cash out, and when she saw all the clothes that I had already put on the counter, her mouth dropped. I acted like I didn't see her expression and got a bag for the clothes that she walked in with.

I was trying to give her time to get to know me before I took shit to another level. I could get my dick wet at any time of the day, but I wanted Crimson. It was time for me to stop playing and give her the dick. Dressing her like this has fucked my head up for real. I always knew she had something good under her clothes, but fuck a snack. Shorty had an entire meal, and I was ready to sit at the table and eat dinner. I glanced at her for the hundredth time. It was amazing what clothes could do for a person.

"You cool with kicking it with me in the hood for a little while?" I asked her.

"I'm fine with whatever you want to do," she replied while looking out the window. Crimson was everything I wanted in a female, but could she be what I needed.

"I have a question, but I don't want you to get offended when I ask you." I cut my eyes at her.

"If you don't want me to take it the wrong way then make sure you deliver it the right way." She pursed her mouth making the perfect O then looked out of the window.

"You are not like the other dudes I met that are in the streets." She stopped talking.

"Is there a question somewhere in that?" She was beating around the bush, and I was tired of waiting for her.

"Just speak your mind. If we're going to be together, you can't be scared to talk to me." She cleared her throat.

"How did you end up here?" She moved her hands in the air. I knew what she really wanted to ask me. How did I end up in the game?

Coming up a nigga like myself never had it easy, but it wasn't that hard either. I wish I could say that I chose the game, but that would be a lie. It was basically handed down to me.

Growing up, my mother wasn't around, I wish I could say she was an alcoholic or drug addict, but that was far from the truth. To be honest, she was just a free spirit, and she wasn't letting her kids hold her back. My grandmother tried to keep her on the up and up, but that didn't go too well though. At the age of fourteen, my mother had her first child, my big brother Tan. She ran away from my grandmother swearing that Tan's father would take care of her and the baby.

Three years later, she popped up asking my grandmother to watch Tan and didn't return. When she finally showed back up to the house, she was twenty years old holding a baby that was three days old. She dumped me on my granny with the diaper I had on and one bottle. She told her that she wasn't made to be a mother. She went about her life as if we never existed, and we probably wouldn't know each other if she walked passed me on the streets.

As we got older, Tan was selling bags. Bags turned into ounces, and ounces eventually turned into bricks. The next thing I knew, my brother was moving more weight than anyone else throughout the city. He moved up so quick that by the time I turned fourteen, I was driving to the surrounding cities delivering bricks for him.

"I started out making runs for my brother. He was doing big things out here. The only thing was that my brother was ruthless about minor shit. So, just imagine if they actually deserved his wrath. He went to the club with this chick he had been talking to. They got drunk, went to the hotel that night, and we found his body at the hotel three days later. After I tied up some loose ends, I tried to turn everything over to Rush, but the connect wouldn't work with him. I stepped back in, and with the help of a couple of vets that ran the hood back in the day, I changed the game, hence the name G or God. They called my brother Satan or Tan for short."

I pulled over and watched her expression as she took in everything. Her expressions went from curious, to scared, to enlightened. I knew she had something else to say, so even though we were at our destination, I waited for her.

"What's so godly about you? I don't get it." She wouldn't get it right off being a church girl.

"My brother bullied people into doing what he wanted. If you told him no there would be a price to pay. If he didn't bully you, it was some form of manipulation going on, and all he did was take. He never gave a person shit. If he helped you, he had some type of ulterior motive behind it. I, on the other hand, gave people a choice. If the same neighborhood I was destroying with drugs needed something done, I made it happen. No one under eighteen can work for me, and if I see potential in them to do better for themselves, I make their ass go to school. I may be young, but I have funded the education for plenty of young people around here. I don't use people kids against them as manipulation tactics, or any of their family members for that matter. I run my shit like a business and take care of my own. No one crosses me because everyone respects me."

She nodded her head understanding what I was saying.

"So, is Major your real brother?" I nodded my head at her.

"Although she knew she wasn't meant to be a mother, it didn't stop her from having Major. He was a drop-off kid just like Tan and me." She played with her fingers, and I could tell that she was nervous about the next question.

"Spit it out so that we can get in here."

"If someone crosses you, what do you do then?"

I closed my eye and tucked my bottom lip thinking about how I would deliver this to her. I couldn't just tell her that when needed to I wouldn't hesitate to put a bullet in a nigga or bitch's head.

"Unlike God, I'm not that forgiving. He gives you chance after chance, but you only have one time with me."

After I answered her question, I got out of the car and went to open her door. It was time to get to this kickback. Plus, Rush had texted me a couple of times asking where we were.

We walked in the house and Keyionte' ran up to Crimson hugging her. I grabbed Crimson's hand because tonight she was with me. She could hang out with her friend anytime. We went right to the smoke room, and Rush was already in there.

"What's good, bruh? I see you got your lady right." He smiled at her eyeballing her body, and I wanted to take his head off.

"Worry about yours, not mine," I told him curtly then shook up with him.

I sat in a chair, pulling Crimson into my lap possessively. I pulled out some weed. Sitting it on the table, I broke down a blunt. Crimson picked it up and began to roll up for me.

"You smoking now?" Keyionte' asked walking up, leaning against Rush. Crimson shook her head no.

"Quinton taught me how to roll up for him. I'm a good passenger, and I can't have him trying to do this while he is driving."

Keyionte' watched her while she pearled for me. When she was done, she inspected it, smiled a little, and then handed it to me. I gave her a quick kiss, and she got up. She and Keyionte' then walked away talking shit.

"Only you can turn a god-fearing woman into that." Major walked into the room shaking up with everybody until he got to the table that Rush and I were at. We all laughed, and I watched my brother stare at the retreating frames of the two women.

I knew who he had his eyes on. Ever since Rush brought Keyionte' around, Major has had a little thing for her. He would never cross the invisible lines that were drawn, but I knew he wanted her. I also knew that Rush would eventually fuck up because he always did. The nigga never knew how to treat women.

A few minutes went by, and we heard yelling, so we all jumped up running to where we heard all the noise coming from.

SEVEN

Keyionte'

"I see G got you right."

I checked my girl out from head to toe. Having a street nigga was doing her some good. He was pulling her out of her shell, and she was becoming the woman that I knew she could be. Don't get me wrong she was still the church girl I had come to know and love. She just had a little edge to her.

She was rocking five-inch stilettos with a pair of jeans and showing a little stomach. Her naturally red hair was in a sleek ponytail, but the end of it was a mass of curls. She still wouldn't swear, and I was fine with that. I just wanted her to find out who she really was without her father being there with what he wanted for her. This girl didn't have a rebellious bone in her body and would follow her father to hell if he led her there. I was the type that if I were going to hell, it would be on my own accord and not because that's where my parents wanted me to go.

"Damn bitch, you can't walk and talk at the same time?"

Before Crimson could open her mouth to add to our conversation, one of the chicks from around here had bumped into her so hard that she fell into me. I knew her being here with G would cause a problem, especially after he has taken her on a little shopping trip and switched her attire up. Bitches are bound to be jealous when real street royalty comes up on a female that's not them. Every bitch in here pussy pulsates for niggas like Quinton, Rush, and Major. For Quinton and Rush to find chicks from the burbs and bring them here is adding insult to injury.

"Was that really called for?" Crimson asked the girl right before her hand came crashing down to Crimson's face.

I felt bad for my girl. She didn't know the rules to this game like I did. Crimson smacked the bitch though and made me proud. That shit was short-lived, and I knew what time it was. Before homegirl could swing on her, I had pushed Crimson behind me and started swinging on every bitch that was close enough to get hit. Crimson stayed with me swinging as best as she could, but these hoes were getting the best of her.

"What the fuck?" Rush yelled out.

I felt the crowd move, but I kept swinging. I wasn't for none of this shit. I heard shit getting knocked over and bitches yelling left and right before I was being picked up off my feet. That didn't have shit to do with my hands though. I was punching bitches as I was being carried away.

"Put that hoe back down. We got shit to settle."

Whoever was holding me let my feet hit the floor and Crimson was standing next to me. They had fucked my friend up, but I had to give her an A for effort. She couldn't fight worth shit, but she was by my side ready for whatever.

"Y'all wanted her now what?" Rush told them.

I knew exactly who was standing behind me, so as long as they had us from behind, I knew I could handle the front of us. Like ten girls stepped up, and I knew most of them which meant that I had more than likely hit when whoever was pulling me out of the crowd. I took a deep breath and squared up, and then I saw a shadow come up next to me.

"What are you doing, nigga?" Rush asked with a hint of laughter in his voice.

"I ain't never about to let ten bitches jump on one and a fourth of people." I raised my eyebrow at Major.

"What do you mean? It's two of them." Quinton was just as curious as the rest of us.

"Nigga, these hands are bisexual, and somebody has to come out here to save sis man. She's trying, but shit is just not working out for her."

Even Crimson had to laugh at that. True to his word, Major stood between Crimson and me knocking bitches out until it was one left. I handled that bitch, and we all were walking out of the house.

~

We all sat in Major's house kicking it drinking and smoking, of course, everyone except Crimson.

"Yo, let me talk to you." Rush had pulled me up off the couch, and I could tell he had an attitude about something.

He led me to a back room. Once he opened the door, he slung me into the room. He grabbed me before I stumbled to the door slamming me against the wall so hard that I heard the wall cracking behind me.

"You think I don't see the way that nigga is looking at you?" he smacked me, making me instantly become dizzy.

"His girl is sitting next to me. Are you sure he wasn't looking at her?" I asked him a logical question. We both knew Major was looking at me though.

"Now you are calling me a liar. You must hate living?" Rush asked me.

I knew not to answer his ass. He was a nut job. Sometimes he would be the most loving person you could ever meet, and minutes later, he's mad and ready to take my head off my shoulders. It was damn near like he was two people inside of one person. His voice even slightly changed. I swallowed hard and thought about what was coming out of my mouth before I said something that would get my ass beat in front of my friends.

"That's not what I'm saying. All I'm saying is that you could be mistaken," I responded weakly.

The look in his eyes let me know that I had fucked up, I tried to brace myself for the smack or punch I knew was coming. He gave me an evil smile then pushed me into the wall so hard I felt my back pop. I wanted to scream from the pain, but I knew better

"Then, you let that nigga stand next to you and fight for you."

Rush started punching me in the ribs, and when I folded, he held me up only to give me a couple of kidney shots. I whimpered. I knew not to get loud. He had slapped me a couple of times before choked me here and there, but never anything like this.

"You belong to me. Always remember that. Everything you have is mine— your body, your mind, and even your fucking soul is mine. I didn't give you life, but always remember I will take that motherfucker." He pulled his dick out of his pants then snatched my pants down. I lay there it felt like I was having an out-of-body experience.

He tried to force himself in me, but my pussy would not submit to him. *Did he really think whipping my ass like this would turn me on?*

"Open up, bitch. If I were that nigga Major your pussy would be like Niagara Falls right now." He tried to ram into me again. It was as if my honeypot had lockjaw. She was not going. It only made him madder, and he smacked me so hard in the face that I blacked out.

I woke up screaming, feeling like I was being ripped in two. This nigga showed me no mercy as he slammed into my back door.

"Open this door now!"

He heard Crimson yelling and banging on the door. I wanted to tell her it was okay, but through my own pain and screams, it was nothing I could do. Rush ignored it all, and he kept going like this shit was okay.

EIGHT

Crimson

I heard the bumping and looked at both Quinton and Major.

"That has nothing to do with you," Quinton told me. Since I didn't hear anything else, I sat back. If nothing else Keyionte' could handle herself.

"What were you about to do anyway pull his hair?" Major said through his laughter. I looked over at Quinton, and he was laughing too. I didn't care though. I stood up for myself even if I got beat up doing it.

"Seriously though, I have to get you in some kickboxing classes or something. You can't be with me and be out here getting your ass beat, bae." I nodded my head at him.

"Maybe you just need to teach her how to shoot." Major still had jokes. He and his girl were both laughing now.

"That's not a bad idea."

Quinton was in deep thought, and as I was about to disagree with him Keyionte' screamed at the top of her lungs. I jumped up running through the hallway opening a couple of doors trying to find her. When I realized what room she was in, I began to beat on it.

"Open this door!" I yelled and started to kick it.

Keyionte' was still screaming, I was thinking about so much stuff that he could be in there doing to her. I just knew he was in there stabbing her or had a gun to her head.

"OPEN THIS FUCKING DOOR!" I yelled.

Quinton and Major both looked at me with their mouths gaped. I couldn't believe the swear word left my mouth, but it felt so good to express it. I started beating and kicking on the door as my heart thudded in my chest. I hadn't heard movement in the room, so everything in me told me that Keyionte' was hurt bad.

About two minutes went by after I swore, and it felt like forever. Rush opened the door looking down on me like he was ready to beat me up. Quinton pushed me past him into the room, and when my eyes fell on Keyionte', I ran to the bed almost dropping to my knees. She was naked and not moving.

"What did you do to her?" I had started sobbing so hard that I was shaking. I had never felt this much anger in my life. I stalked up to him, and he turned toward me like he was ready to treat me like he had Keyionte'.

"Get your bihh…" Rush never got the words out before Quinton punched him in the mouth.

"Get the fuck out!" Major had stepped between Rush and Quinton.

Rush turned to leave the house without looking back. Quinton turned going in the opposite direction of the room. Major, on the other hand, was right behind me. I quickly covered Keyionte' up.

"I need a cold towel," I told Major. Instead of him going to get it, he carefully picked Keyionte' up carrying her to the nearest bathroom. I stood looking at the bed full of blood.

"She's bleeding!" I yelled to Major's back.

I walked in the bathroom, and he was sitting on the toilet with Keyionte' completely wrapped up on his lap. Her head hung backwards.

"Run a warm bath."

I went to the bathtub doing as he told me. My hands were shaking so bad that I could barely complete the task. It felt like hours had passed, and she still hadn't come out of it. Major's little friend came to the door looking in, and I could tell from her expression she didn't like what she was seeing.

"Go the fuck home," Major told her without looking up.

He placed Keyionte' in the tub as if she was a porcelain doll. His friend stared at him and Keyionte' for a minute before she reluctantly turned her back to us and walked away. Major took the towel placing it over Keyionte's forehead, and she woke up swinging. He whispered something in her ear, and she quickly calmed down.

"You know you don't have to take this shit, right?" Major told her in a low soft tone.

Tears began to roll down Keyionte' bruised and battered face. My heart broke for my friend, even going through what she had just gone through with Rush I knew she wasn't going to leave him alone just yet.

"Let me drop you off." Quinton walked up behind me pulling me into his chest.

I knew Keyionte' was safe with Major, and I wouldn't have to worry about her. I turned giving Quinton a full-on hug. Him standing behind me with a full erection against my behind had me thinking about everything.

"But Keyionte'…" I pointed at my friend as tears rolled down her face. This situation had me heartbroken.

"I got her. Y'all can go ahead," Major told us while keeping my eyes on Keyionte'. Quinton pulled me out of the bathroom by my hand.

"Yo, G you know you're going to have to keep eyes on Rush." Major gave us a serious expression.

"I got it, bruh," Quinton replied pulling me through the hallway.

NINE

Rush

"Who the fuck do these niggas think they are getting in my fucking business?" I questioned myself looking around the living room of my bitch Gina's house.

"What you say, babe?"

I turned towards Gina with fury radiating off my body. She stopped instantly and started shaking. I gave her an evil grin, and she ran to her room closing the door slamming it. Standing in the middle of the floor, I couldn't believe that my niggas who I grew up with were about to let a couple of hoes come between us, and one of them was mine.

I saw how Major kept his eyes on Keyionte' like she was up for grabs. The nigga had me fucked up if he thought he was about to ease in on my territory. Keyionte' was mine, and they knew how I felt about my women, once mines always mine. My bitches may as well consider themselves marked. If I were a dog and pissed on a fire hydrant, no other dog would dare piss in my spot. That was all me, and my niggas knew it.

~

I started pacing the floor trying to figure out how I got to Gina's house and trying not to listen to the voices taking over my mind telling me to set this house on fire. Something was wrong, and I couldn't figure out what it was.

"You have to kill Quinton and Major."

I shook my head trying to clear it of the voices that were speaking to me.

Quinton is my nigga. We came up together running packs for his brother Tan. Once Tan was killed, I was supposed to take over, but the bitches in the mob didn't want to fuck with me, so Quinton ended up having to step back in the game. The mob has had no contact with me at all. When Quinton goes to handle business, Major is by his side each time. It's as if Quinton told the mob that I'm kind of fucked up in the head or something because they have nothing to do with me.

"Naw, he wouldn't do that. He didn't even tell Tan that I was fucked up, so I know he won't tell an outsider," I spoke aloud to myself as I leaned back on the couch, laying my head back closing my eyes.

"Yes, he did."

I opened my eyes looking around for the person that said that only to find no one.

"That's your brother from another mother. He wouldn't do that."

I tried to be content with the last statement.

"Damn, this shit is getting worse. Maybe I need to try and get some help for this," I voiced out loud.

I knew what it was. My mother suffered from the same sickness that I'm going through right now. I just feel like I have some extra shit going on in my head. There have been times that I didn't recall doing some shit, but everyone else said I did. It was like I had mini blackouts or something. They say if a person tells you they're crazy, they're really not. However, I knew I was a half a step away from the white padded room.

"Gina, bring your ass out here and give me some head girl. Come sit on this motherfucker or something."

Gina peeped her head out of the door like she was scared to

walk through her own house. I watched her as she cautiously walked up to me going down on her knees. Her lip quivered a little like she didn't want to fuck with me.

"What's wrong, ma? You just gone sit there like you're scared to touch me?" Her body began to shake, and she was on the brink of tears.

I pulled my dick out to show her how hard my shit was and why I wanted her to stop playing with me like she didn't know what to do with it. Her eyes got big, and she backed away from me. I looked down at my dick covered in blood and shit.

What the fuck did I do? The thought crossed my mind right before everything faded to black.

TEN

Crimson

"Wake up babe. You're home."

I opened my eyes taking in my surroundings, realizing I was in front of my house. Tonight's events had worn me out, not to mention the adrenaline rush from the fight and stuff that went on with Keyionte' was long gone. My muscles ached like never before, my vision was blurred from being hit in the eye, and my lips and jaw were swollen. I really needed to learn how to fight. Being with a man like Quinton came with some complications. I turned to look at him, giving him a weak smile. I know I looked like I was run over by a truck, but he wasn't looking at me any different from any other day.

"I'm sorry I messed up the party."

I knew all of this was far from being my fault, but I still felt a little responsible for some of the confusion I had gotten into. Who would have thought a day of chilling with my guy, shopping, and going to a party would end like this? Even though I got beat up pretty bad, for some reason, fighting over Quinton was worth it all. He wasn't the kind of guy I was used to dating, but he was by far the best. He had more manners and charm then half of the godly men I had dated before him.

"Ain't none of the shit that happened tonight on you ma, except for maybe getting your ass beat like that. I thought you would have at least known how to throw a fucking punch with Keyionte' being your friend." He paused staring at me bewildered.

If he only he knew that all of the fights that I may have had growing up. Keyionte' was the one out there throwing the punches. Besides tonight, I have never had to raise my hand in my life. Keyionte' always protected me from the girls that were mad about my beauty, complexion, and crimson colored hair. Heck, I don't even think I could do a good windmill if needed.

"First thing first, I'm signing you up for some type of self-defense class Monday. Also, you'll be taking a firearms class, and you're doing target practice with me or Major three times a week." He gave me a look like what he was saying was set in stone.

"I have a job, so I don't know if I can pull all that off." I adjusted myself in the seat so that I can be eye to eye with him. I know he didn't expect me to quit my job just to run behind him. I cleared my throat to voice my opinion about his plan.

"You need to find a way around it. Even if we never talk again in this lifetime, you need to be able to protect yourself. At the rate Keyionte' is going, she won't be around to protect you all the time," he stated before I could say anything.

"What I am supposed to do, lie to my father about why I am not at work?" He raised a quizzical brow at me.

"You're a grown ass woman Crimson, figure this shit out."

I closed my eyes taking a deep breath. He didn't understand the way I was raised. I was taught to obey my father's rules until I was married off and living with my husband. Quinton wasn't a part of my life's plan. He just kind of fell in my lap. I could sit here and go back and forth with him, but he lived by his own rules. He said it himself. He was God in these streets, and I was just a church girl from the suburbs. He was out here pretending to be the higher power. I didn't want to argue with him though. I was tired of fighting and today has been nothing but a fight.

I was already going behind my father's back being with him, hanging in his hood, and the clothes I had on were sure to get me fussed at if my father saw me in them. I needed him to understand that I was held at a different standard than the average young woman. I am the daughter of a prominent black preacher, and I was expected to walk, talk, and dress according to those standards.

I didn't want to argue, so I moved over closer to him practically in his lap placing my lips on his and ignoring the pain that was shooting through them as I kissed my man. I would find a way to make what he wanted me to do happen. In a matter of months, this man had become my world, and I couldn't imagine my life without him after being with him.

Our kiss started so soft then got hotter and heavier. Quinton brought his hands up my legs kneading them before sliding his hands in my pants and massaged my clit through my panties. I know he felt the moisture of my wetness through my panties. He moved my them to the side and inserted his finger in me pulling it out and placing it in his mouth, then kissing me so that I could taste my own juices. This man could have anything I own. Before I was able to pull away from our kiss to let him know what I was thinking, I was being snatched from the truck by one leg and one arm.

"What the hell are you doing out here with this nig… I mean man?" My father had a death grip on my arm.

"Daddy wait, let me explain." My father who had never laid a hand on me in my life was shaking the mess out of me.

"Let you explain what? How you've been out here fornicating with this hoodlum." The waterworks were coming for the second time tonight. Out of all the people that could have walked up on me at this moment why him?

"Dad, he's my man, not a hoodlum!" I yelled. Quinton had gotten out the car, but I could tell he was skeptical about stepping between a father and daughter.

"Sir, can you please stop shaking her like that."

My dad turned on his heels, and I knew it was going to be some shit. My dad was far from a punk, but I knew for a fact Quinton wasn't to be played with. He was soft on me and with me, but not so much to grown men like my father. My dad had a way of trying to bully people into getting them to do what he wanted, but Quinton was one man it wouldn't be working on. It was then that I realized I might be the one that caused my father to get killed in front of his own home and I wouldn't be able to say anything about it because the man I loved would be the one to do it.

"Don't tell me how to treat my damn child."

My mouth dropped at my father's choice of words. I had never heard anything close to profanity come out of his mouth except the word hell, and he was referring to the place at those times. I was so struck dumb that I hadn't realized that my dad was taking steps closer to Quinton. I ran between them placing a hand upon my dad's chest. I couldn't let this happen. However, what was I supposed to do when I had two men over six feet towering over me ready to come to blows?

"Dad, step back." My father halted his steps, taking a good look at me for the first time.

"You're putting your fucking hands on my daughter?" My dad charged at Quinton slinging me to the ground without a second thought.

I could see the steam coming off both of them, and this was sure to end in a blood bath. I let out a piercing scream. Quinton dodged my dad's punch, and he slammed my father straight into the truck. Quinton kneeled to help me up looking me over to make sure I was okay. My dad started fumbling around his waist for something as Quinton pulled his gun out and had it aimed at my father.

"What the fuck are you doing?" I questioned Quinton, feeling my anger rising. I was ready to explode. How fucking dare he pull out a gun on my father?

I raised my hand to smack him and stopped short when I saw the look in his eyes and heard something hit the concrete behind me. I turned to see a gun on the ground next to my father's feet.

"You were going to shoot him?" I stormed up to my dad. I had to get this shit under control, or one of them would end up in someone's morgue.

"You worried about some little punk ass nigga that can't keep his hands to himself? He doesn't even respect you if he beats on you. Now you have him out here ready to shoot me because you can't keep your fucking legs closed. You think I didn't see him digging all in your ass before I snatched you out of that truck." He paused, waving his hands like a lunatic. "I swear I have done my best by you. I've kept you away from his kind for a reason. I should've known that no matter what I did you would still grow up to become a whore just like your mother and her mother. Your grandmother told me as soon as you were born to be careful because being a whore was genetic. With me thinking that I could save you from the world, I didn't listen. You have broken my heart, and I'm ashamed of you."

My dad's words hit me like a ton of bricks. Did he really think that low of me?

"You fucking my whore of mother doesn't say much about you now, does it? I have lived my life according to your rules and the life plans that you have laid out for me. I must commend you. After all that I have done to make you proud, I have to say that no one has ever made me feel as demoralized as you have right this moment."

I couldn't stop the tears that were coming down my face. My father had done something he told me never to let any man do, which was break my heart. He stood there looking at me like I had stolen from his grandmother and was the lowest dirtiest thing he had ever seen in his life. I wish I had the power to become invisible. I felt the lowest I have ever felt in my life.

"Off the strength of your daughter, I won't kill you. Know there's never been a time that I pulled my gun and didn't bust it so consider yourself lucky. By the way, I never laid a hand on your daughter, next time you see Keyionte' ask her why Crimson came home like that."

"Let's go Quinton."

He kept his gun aimed at my father while getting in the truck with a smirk on his face. Dang even when my world is falling apart that man's facial expressions bring me some type of joy. I stood at the passenger side of the truck staring at my father and making sure he didn't pick his gun up off the ground.

"I pray to God…" Quinton and I both started laughing cutting off the rest of his sentence.

I got in the truck, and Quinton pulled off. I watched the dumbfounded expression on my dad's face until I couldn't see him anymore. My heart was broken. I had chosen to leave what I had known my entire life for the unknown with a man that I had been with for a few months. Was he worth going into war with my father? I closed my eyes gathering my thoughts. I had been through more today than I had been through in my entire life. I let my mind drift off over the years of being under my father's wings.

When I opened my eyes after we took the short ride to Quinton's house realizing that I hadn't chosen Quinton over my father, I had chosen myself. After tonight, my life would change. I was a little leery about the outcome, but then again how could I be when I was in control of everything.

ELEVEN

Keyionte'

"You don't have to knock on the door, Major. Just come in!" I yelled from the room he had let me use while I healed up.

I was glad that Major let me stay at his house while I got well. The nigga made sure I had everything I needed. I was scared to go back home. I didn't want to explain what happened to my parents. Plus, Rush would have caught me coming out of the house and probably abducted my ass.

Whoever was at the door knocked again. Major would have come in by now, so I knew it wasn't him. I walked over to the door. Swinging it open, Crimson and Quinton were standing in front of me.

"Wait a minute." I closed the door putting a shirt over my sports bra that covered the booty shorts I had on. I opened the door back up stepping back so that they could come in. Crimson walked in plopping down on the bed, and Quinton stood in the door.

"What's going on, chick?" Crimson asked me while looking me over.

"I'm good, getting better. I'm glad I'm healing quick because my parents are having a fit." I walked over to the bed sitting beside her.

"I just wanted to see if you were good. Major and I are about to handle some business. Don't let anybody in this house." Quinton smiled at Crimson before walking away, and she blushed.

"What's up with that?" I asked her, smiling. This was a part of my bestie that I hadn't seen before. She had a glow about her that only a man can put on a woman's face, she looked happy and that made me happy.

"Nothing really, nothing has changed except my living situation." I felt like my eyes were about to pop out of my head from her admission.

"So that's why my parents were asking me all of those questions. They asked me about your face and swore that Quinton was beating the shit out of you." Crimson rolled her eyes.

"If you only knew the half of it. I heard and saw my father do some things that night that I didn't know he was capable of. Can you believe he tried to pull a gun on Quinton?"

I spit out the water I had just drunk. What the fuck was going on?

"What?" Crimson folded her arms and rolled her eyes.

"Girl, my father acted a damn fool that night. He called my phone leaving me messages for a few days telling me how I was going to hell if I didn't come back to the house. I'm guessing whatever you told your parents must be what stopped him from calling and texting. What did you tell them?" she questioned me like I had performed a miracle.

"I told them the truth about what happened that night except what happened to me." I cleared my throat so that I wouldn't cry.

"How are you doing?" she grabbed my hand, squeezing it.

"I'm making it. I can't lie. Major is a great help." I hugged myself before continuing.

"Are you going back?" I could tell that she already had answered that question in her head.

"I need you to understand that Rush isn't a bad nigga. It's just that sometimes he seems like a different person. The shit just happens all of a sudden at times. Honestly, I don't know what I would do once that time comes."

Crimson nodded her head at me, but she had a sorrowful expression on her face. I knew she wouldn't understand what I was feeling. She had the good nigga out of the friends.

"Whatever happens just know I'm here for you." She leaned over hugging me, and I knew what she had told me was true. Crimson and I were sisters. No matter what happened, we would be here for each other through thick and thin.

We chilled in the room for a couple of hours then got up to make something to eat before both of our phones went off at the same time. Crimson grabbed her phone reading a text, and I answered mine.

"Yeah." I stood at the counter listening to Major as he told me what was going on. I rolled my eyes up to the ceiling and said a silent prayer.

When he hung up, I ran to his room getting everything he told me to grab, including his keys to his Range Rover. I turned to look at Crimson. I could tell she was mad as hell and her father had really just lost her forever with this stunt.

"Who was the text from?" I questioned because I knew it wasn't Quinton. He was being held in jail for abducting Crimson.

I shook my head. What the hell was Rev thinking about doing this shit? I guess I would never know the feeling of being a desperate parent until I actually have children, I wasn't looking forward to that in any way. Although I was a good child for my parents, I was sneaky as hell.

"That was my dad telling me that he reported me missing and gave the police Quinton's plate number." She was stomping out of the door going to the car. This shit had to give.

TWELVE

Quinton

"Where's Crimson Anderson?"

I sat in the interrogation room with my hands cuffed to the table watching the detectives play good cop bad cop for the last hour. If I weren't on the other side of this shit, it would be comical. I couldn't hold my laughter in any longer. I let that shit flow freely. They both looked at me like I had lost my mind.

"You think this is shit a joke?" Detective Ford slammed his hands down on the table like it was supposed to put some kind of fear into me.

"Hell yeah, it's funny as fuck. You two actually need your own TV show." I laughed at them again. The good cop, Detective Miller, came charging towards me. Ford grabbed him quick slamming him against the wall.

"Be cool, man," Ford told him. I gave his ass a crooked smile. I had got to his ass.

"I feel like y'all need to get a room from all this touching and role-playing y'all doing." Ford walked up to me and punched me in the mouth. I tasted the saltiness of my blood in my mouth and spat on the floor.

"We have someone that stated they saw you holding Crimson at gunpoint until she got in the car with you. Laugh now, but you will not be leaving here anytime soon." Detective Miller stared me down.

I knew Crimson would be here soon, so I decided to play with them a little bit.

"You all are right. There's no need for me to waste your time. I did take her at gunpoint, and you all will never find her." Their faces fell like they had just cracked the case of their careers.

"We need that in writing," Detective Ford quickly stated, grabbing some paper like he was about to have me sign my life away. Little did they know the joke was on them.

They took my hands out of the cuffs, and it took everything in me not to get my fucking lick back off Miller. I would find his ass and let that bastard know he wasn't untouchable. I rubbed my wrist to get the circulation back flowing into my hands. I pulled the paper to me acting like I was writing my statement out, and once I put my signature to it, the door to the room opened.

"Let's go, Quinton." I stood up smiling at my lawyer and the officer that walked him to the back.

"What do you mean let's go? He just gave us a statement that he abducted Crimson Anderson and we would never find her?" Detective Ford picked up the piece of paper that I had written on, and his face turned red.

"Well, he lied. Crimson is in the lobby talking to one of our people and her father." I laughed walking out of the door. This shit couldn't have gone any better if I planned it.

"What was on the paper he gave you?" I heard the officer ask. I laughed as I thought of the sentence that I had written down several times. *Fuck both of you gay bitches, and you hit like a bitch.*

"Why in the hell would you lie like that daddy? Do you know how many innocent black men get killed for nothing?" My laughter was short-lived when I heard Crimson yelling. I began to pick up my pace to get to her.

"My daughter needs some help. She has Stockholm's Syndrome." I took a deep breath hearing the old man rant. In his eyes, Crimson was brainwashed.

"There's nothing wrong with me, but evidently something is wrong with you. I had forgotten my gun in the car that they were driving. This could've gone so bad." Crimson was shaking her head and rubbing her temples, and I could tell that she was stressed.

"It wouldn't have been no better for him."

I bald my fist up, and I was ready to kill this old man. Fuck him being her father. Crimson stood in front of him like he had smacked her in the face, and I could tell that she was playing the words over in her head trying to compute a reaction to his words.

"WHAT THE FUCK!!!" she yelled lunging up at her father.

Major grabbed her around her waist picking her up off her feet and turning in the opposite direction. She kicked and screamed obscenities that I had never heard out of her mouth before. One week living with me and I had turned her vocabulary from good girl to sailor language. She was going so hard that she was making shit up to call her father. I was happy that she was going that hard for me, but this was a sad sight to see. I knew she loved her dad and her reaction to him at this moment was all of his fault, but he was fucking up his relationship with his daughter so bad.

"Calm down, Crimson. Yes, this shit could've been avoided, but Quinton is okay," Major told her.

Although his voice was calm, the look in his eyes told a story of a killer. Crimson's dad had crossed a line trying to take out the family, and Major was ready to get his hands on this man. Crimson wasn't trying to hear him. Her no fighting ass was on attack mode, and it was turning me on like a motherfucker.

"How dare you speak to me like that? I am your father. If you would've done what I said and left this nigga alone, we wouldn't be here right now. Just so you know, I won't stop until you are back in your right mind." Her father stood there smugly.

"Fuck you, Joel!" Crimson yelled out, and her father charged toward the three of them. Before he could get close to Major with his back turned, I had gotten between them, grabbed him by the neck, and lifted him in the air slamming him onto the floor.

"Nigga, don't make me kill you about mine. I'm trying to be

nice." I got up dusting myself off before the police could grab me. I grabbed Crimson from Major.

"Calm down, ma. I'm okay." I pulled her close to me then headed for the door. I had been in this place longer then I wanted to.

"Oh my God..." I knew her father was about to finish his sentence, but I couldn't resist.

"What?" I turned to look at him with a smirk on my face as he stood there with a confused expression.

"Come on, God," Crimson said grabbing my hand completely pulling me out of the doors.

She had never addressed me as God or G before, so I knew she only did that because of her father. Although I could tell that she is breaking apart inside from this entire situation, I had to give it to my baby because she held her shit together until we walked through the door of our house.

Crimson walked into the house straight to the bedroom and fell on the bed. She was crying so hard she was shaking. She turned her back to me not wanting me to see her like this. If it were any other bitch, I would have walked away from them, but I couldn't do that to Crimson. I can't say that I was used to dealing with crying women. I kicked off my shoes, walked to the other side of the bed, laid down, and pulled her close to me.

"It's okay, ma. You are going to always be good. I know it hurts, and you can't see it right now, but I got you. You will never have to worry about shit, okay."

She nodded her head as she soaked my shirt with tears. It felt like she cried for hours when it had only been about a couple of minutes. She lay next to me not saying a word, and then she lifted her head and kissed me.

I kissed her back. When she started going for my zipper, I knew what she wanted. We had danced around having sex since she walked into my house a week ago. I knew she wasn't that experienced, and I couldn't make love to her like most women like her wanted. I am a thoroughbred. Therefore, I fuck.

I rolled over on my back placing her on top of me. If this is what she wanted, she had to get it on her own. She slithered her body down mine, unzipped my pants, pulled my dick out, wrap one hand around my ten inches, and then put her mouth on the head.

My breath caught in my throat as soon as her mouth made contact. Her warm mouth felt like heaven. She sucked it like she was trying to get used to the idea of it, but when she took her mouth all the way down making my wood disappear, I lost my mind. Her mouth was juicy as hell. She then did what I never thought she would do. She spit on my shit, rubbed it with her hand, and then kept sucking.

"Ohh," she hissed out when I grabbed a hand full of her hair, pulling her off my dick.

I flipped Crimson on her back, snatching her jeans and panties off. When my eyes landed on her freshly waxed pussy, I wanted to taste that shit so bad. I bent down, burying my face between her legs, and eating her pussy like it was my last meal. My dick got harder each time I heard a moan leave her mouth. When I felt her about to come, I got up and slammed into her, and Crimson's body convulsed upon impact.

"Yeah baby, come on this dick," I told her pulling out and slamming into her again.

The suction of her pussy was driving me crazy. I stayed in her for a minute before moving, letting her enjoy the moment. I repeated my stroke on her, and she put her hand up trying to hold me back. I moved back and flipped her on her hands and knees, and I pushed her face down to the bed, pulling both of her hands behind her back.

"This is my pussy, and I do what I want to it, you got me?" I made sure I had a good grip on her hands before slamming into her again.

"Ohh," she muffled through the bed.

"Answer me, Crimson." I pulled a hand full of her hair while long stroking her again.

"Yes!" she yelled, and I plunged into her. I was about to come, and although I was aggressive when it came to sex, I wasn't a selfish nigga.

"Come for me, ma."

Her body stiffened, and her pussy put a death grip on me as she flooded my dick with her juices. Fuck! She was a squirter. I came as her pussy went crazy coming on me again.

"I told you that pussy was mine," I told her as we lay in bed catching our breath. I had never fucked a bitch that had better pussy then her. That shit had a nigga feeling a certain type of way for real. Crimson moved closer to me, laying her head on my chest.

"We didn't use a condom, and I'm not on birth control. I haven't had a reason to use them since—" She cut off her own sentence, and I pulled her into me.

"It's doesn't matter. You're not going anywhere, and I'm clean," I told her before going to sleep.

THIRTEEN

Major

THREE MONTHS LATER

"Yo, I know I got you this townhouse, but you really don't have to move out of my house," I told Keyionte' as I carried a box into her house.

"Three months is way too long to be living with you. I already feel like I've overstayed my welcome." She sat the bag that she was carrying down putting her hands on her hips, looking at me.

"What would make you say some shit like that? I didn't have a problem with you being there."

I really didn't have a problem with her being there, but once she started stressing about getting her own place, I gave in. I didn't want her to stress about shit. She had already gone through a thing when her parents put her out once Crimson's dad told them she helped attack him. Who the fuck knew a preacher could lie that fucking much? Better yet who knew that her parents would actually listen to his conniving ass.

"You haven't said anything, but the day your bitch was here and saw me in the kitchen with my bra and panties on, she made it very clear." I furrowed my eyebrows at her.

"Why didn't you say anything then? I would've kicked that bitch out with nothing on. It wasn't her business why you were in there like that. You should've told her she was a visitor in your house, and she could get the fuck out."

Keyionte' shook her head at me.

"That's the thing, Major. It wasn't my house. It is yours."

She was standing in front of me like she had made a valid point; anywhere I lived could be hers. I fucks with shorty the long way, and the only reason that I hadn't come at her was because of what Rush did to her. I felt like she needed time to heal from the wounds that we couldn't see. I know that crazy nigga switched up on her so quickly that she didn't know what the fuck happened. Rush needs to take meds for his shit, but he refused to, and since we've grown up together, we would never leave him out here like that. He had at least five people living inside of him that Quinton and I had met so far. We were cool with all them, so we never had to worry about him switching up on us, until the day he raped Keyionte'.

When Crimson got in his face, we thought Killa was going to take her out, and there was no way Quinton or I was about to let that happen. With the look he gave us, I swear I thought I was going to have to empty my magazine on him. He thought better of the situation and left when I told him to. This was the exact reason the cartel didn't want to fuck with him when Tan died. Quinton had suggested leaving the game and Rush taking over, but they weren't going for that it. I guess Tan had told them how crazy he was, or they had eyes on them because they told Quinton that they would shut down everything if he left.

To be honest, I'm glad they did because Killa is worse than Tan in some ways, and he would've been out here shooting everybody because the wind blew.

"I just don't get why you wanted to move you were much safer at the house with me, but in a way, I get it."

Keyionte' was ready to start over without Rush and all the people living in his head. Also, I knew she wasn't ready for anything with me. She had never been out here on her own like that, and I wanted her to get the chance to know what it felt like. I had been out here living by myself since I was twelve. Quinton and Tan took care of the things I needed, but when it came to daily living, those niggas were nowhere to be found. I moved into a condo thirteen, I purchased my townhouse at seventeen with my own money . My granny was getting too old to chase behind me, so they put me up in my own spot.

"Okay I won't bring it up anymore, but I need you to be careful. Sleep with your gun under your pillow. When you go out, have it where you can easily get to it, and if you have to, pull the trigger."

"Don't hesitate and shoot to kill." She repeated what Quinton and I had been telling her and Crimson for the past three months.

I was proud of both of them when it came to target practice. Crimson was learning how to dodge a couple of punches, but to be honest, she was still getting her beat up.

Keyionte' and I finished getting everything moved in and decided to grab something to eat. After ordering in, we sat on her new cream leather couch chilling and talking shit. That's what I loved about her. We could chill like we were homies. She would be the perfect ride or die for me. She had made a couple of runs with me, riding shotgun with the Glock on her lap. What more could I really ask for? I never wanted to step on my nigga Rush toes, but he couldn't handle the woman she is. He would only break her down, and I couldn't let that happen.

I continued to go back and forth in my mind until I leaned over and kissed her.

"What are you doing?" She pulled away from me staring into my eyes. Her mouth said she was confused, but her eyes told a different story.

"Tell me you haven't thought about this and you don't want it, and I'll never come at you again." I could see the wheels spinning in her head.

"What about Rush?" she asked.

I could tell she was concerned, but Rush hadn't been around us like that since he fucked her up. He came and took care of his part of the business, but he left afterward. He wasn't saying too much to us since Quinton told him what would happen to him if he came up on Crimson like that again.

"I'm not ducking that nigga, and you don't have to neither. I'm not about to beg you for shit. Either you want this, or you don't."

She raised her eyebrow at me before coming in close to kiss me. She threw her leg over me straddling me. The little shorts she had on rose up to her ass cheeks, and I didn't hesitate to palm it, pulling her closer.

FOURTEEN

Keyionte'

I locked my lips onto Major's and didn't want to pull back. He deserved to have this and more from me. Major had turned out to be my knight and shining armor after Rush had fucked me up. That nigga took care of me and washed me when I couldn't wash myself. When I woke up screaming in the middle of the night, he made his way to my bedside no matter what hoe he had in the house with him, and if a bitch looked at me crazy while there, he showed her the door. I owe this man my sanity for real. He was everything that I wanted and needed.

I knew the day of Major and me fucking around would come. I just didn't know when. He used to walk around the house in basketball shorts with no shirt on showing off everything. I had never seen a soft dick so big until I saw him, but what got me was when he had company, and I could hear his females crying out and screaming in passion as his headboard hit up against the wall. That shit was a straight turn on for me, and I wanted to walk in the room and just watch what was going on while playing with my clit to get off. I know this nigga was in that room beasting hoes, and I wanted to be a part of the action.

I straddled Major and rolled my hips against his hardening dick while he groped my ass cheeks. He moved my shorts to the side, and I felt his mouth twitch into a smile when he realized I wasn't wearing any panties. He slid a finger into me, and my pussy gripped his finger. Moving in and out of me, I came on him within a minute. I couldn't remember the last time someone touched me and wasn't being aggressive about it.

Major lifted me off his lap ripping my shorts off then stood up pulling his down. When his dick sprung loose from the confinement of his shorts, my knees damn near buckled. I had never seen a dick so big and pretty in my life. My mouth began to water. He picked me up, and I instantly wrapped my legs around his waist. When he impaled me with his manhood, my breath caught, and I froze coming with his first stroke. *What the fuck was he doing to me?* Major placed my back against the wall, pushing more of his dick into me, and my body reacted the same way.

With another stroke, I felt more dick in me than I thought I could handle. This nigga had to be part horse. He waited for my body to accommodate his size and then went in for the kill. I tried to hold back and not cry out like the hoes I had heard through the walls at his house, but he was more than great at this shit.

He started biting my neck and chest. He moved me to the kitchen island and bit down on my nipple. You would think that it was a turn-off, but everything he did was tied into pleasure. What I loved about him was that he wasn't into talking shit while fucking you, he just showed you better than he could tell you.

"Give me a minute."

We had moved to the bedroom. He had my head spinning, and after an hour of nonstop fucking, I was dehydrated. I lay in bed for a minute trying to get the nerves in my legs together before getting out the bed.

"You okay?" he asked with a smile on his face.

"I'm good, but what I need to know is what drugs are you on that you can go so long without busting a nut." He laughed at me like I had lost my mind.

"I'm not on drugs, and I have nutted in you about three times, I just kept going. Every time I move you from one place to the next, I was getting ready for the next round." I cocked my head at him. He wasn't human. I went to get us something to drink. Going back into the room, I sat on the bed next to him.

"If you don't know it yet, you're my girl, and that whole Rush shit is out of the question."

He didn't have to tell me that. I knew it from the moment he went in me raw. After all that dick he gave me and had me coming more times in one session then I had in my life, Rush was a memory. It's sad to say that dick was the thing that brought me to this point. Once you put that with the fact that he is an all-around good dude, you had my new man.

"I know that, Major. You didn't even have to say it. I might be down for a lot of shit, but I don't fuck more than one person at a time." He nodded his head at me, went into my bag that was on the floor, pulled out both of my guns, and placed one under his pillow and one under mine.

"Come back to bed and get your dick." He laid on his back.

I looked down at his body taking in every muscle and all his tattoos. He had the body of a god with the dick of a stallion. I leaned over him, licked my lips, and placed his dick in my mouth. If it was mine like he said it was, it was only right that I got a taste of it.

A couple of weeks had passed, and Major and I had spent timed between his townhouse and mines. We kept the same vibe. The only thing that had changed was that we were fucking. He was like my male best friend and counterpart. I loved the fact that we were one now. I hadn't heard anything from or about Rush until one day Major and I was at his townhouse knocked out sleep when someone started banging on the door.

"Open the door. We need to talk!"

The banging and yelling continued, but Major was in his nineteenth dream and hadn't heard shit. I shook him, and he mumbled something under his breath. I rolled my eyes. *It doesn't make any sense this nigga sleeps this hard.*

"Get up, Major. Someone's at the door." He finally jumped up pointing his gun towards the bedroom door.

"Nigga, if that were the case, we would be dead because you don't hear anything when you're asleep." He was about to say something slick back, but the pounding on the door started again.

"How long has he been at my door doing this?" I cocked my head at him not believing that someone could go completely deaf in their sleep.

"For about ten minutes, and who the fuck is it?" I asked not recognizing the voice right off. Major got up out the bed putting his basketball shorts on.

"Don't come out of this room or I will end up catching a case, you got me?"

I was caught off guard. We had been all over Chicago together, so why did I have to stay put? Instead of speaking my thoughts, I nodded my head at him. He walked out of the room closing the door. I waited until I heard him open the front door before wrapping my hand around my nine, getting up, and cracking the door. I put my ear to the crack listening to what was going on.

"What's wrong, Killa?" I heard Major say. I had never heard of or saw a nigga named Killa from there crew. Who the fuck was this man that I had to hide?

"I can't find her man."

I heard Rush's voice and damned near pissed on myself. It was crazy because it was like the voice he uses when he's mad but rougher in a way. Why was he calling him Killa? That shit wasn't computing in my head. I shook my head getting out of my own thoughts so that I could listen to this conversation attentively. One or two of the three people in this house was losing their damn mind, and I had to make sure it wasn't me.

"Who?" Major asked. He knew who Rush was looking for just like I did.

Once I decided I wasn't talking to Rush anymore, I changed my number and started knew social media pages under a different name. I didn't have time to play with him.

"I can't find Keyionte'. I need to find her. I love that bitch, and she done cut me off. I figure if I gave her time to get over what I had done to her that she would come back to me. How the fuck she fall off the face of the earth?"

I couldn't believe he thought that I would come back to him after he beat me and literally rammed his dick up my ass. I shuddered at the thought of him doing that to me.

"Let me talk to Rush, yo. You've been out here running around too long," I heard Major say. I didn't understand what was going on, and I didn't know if I wanted to understand it.

"Once I find Keyionte' I will let him out, but not until then." I wanted to fall out. What had I gotten myself into. This nigga was talking about himself in third person.

"Killa, you are tripping man." I listened to them go back and forth.

"How long have I been out?" Rush's voice changed, and when it did, it was like a caress to my skin. How could this shit be happening? Sliding down the wall, I hit the floor, making sure not to make a sound.

"For a couple of months now this time around. You need to get some help for all this shit, man. When you're gone, Killa is doing the most. He's going to land you in jail. Then when you're here most of the time, you hearing voices and shit. I think you need to let us take you to the center, man. I'm worried that one of those voices is going to tell you to kill yourself or another personality might come out and do it for you. When you were going through your spells, I understood why Killa come out, but that nigga is fucked up."

I heard pacing, and I figure it was Rush since Major had just verified that he was certifiable. I could kick myself in the ass for getting into this, and I was going to be all over Major's ass for not telling me Rush was a fucking lunatic.

"Call G tomorrow and set things up for me. I know I have to get this together before I end up killing someone innocent." The footsteps stopped.

"Killa, bring him back man." I could tell Major was mad at the change, and I was freaked the fuck out.

"You know I hear everything y'all say. I will find Keyionte' and disappear before I let y'all put me in a padded room!" Seconds later, the door slammed, and Major was back in the room looking around for me.

"What the hell is going on?" I was still sitting on the floor feeling like a fool. I had been bamboozled, tricked into fucking both of them and loving one of them. Major came and sat on the floor beside me.

"It's really not my story to tell," he said, leaning his head against the wall with his eyes closed like he was exhausted from a ten-minute conversation with one person, or was it two people? I was just as confused as the man that had walked out of the house.

"Right now, I feel like I'm being played, so you need to tell me something."

I started tapping the gun that was still in my hand on the floor. Major opened his eyes looked at me then closed them back. He knew when I was thinking. I tapped my fingers, foot, pen, or whatever I had in my hand at the time. It was like the noise and movement helped me process things better.

"Rush has some issues." He stopped.

"No shit, I knew that after he fucked me up in the other room. Now tell me something I don't know." He opened his eyes staring at me.

"If I hear this shit outside of this house, I swear as much as I love you, I will fuck you up. Before I start, I should let you know if it gets out I will know it's you because no one knows what I'm about to tell you but Quinton and me. Now, do you still want to know?" What the fuck did he think? Rush or Killa wanted to snatch me up.

"I have a right to know what I have gotten myself into. Fuck your code of honor. I'm your bitch. I stopped fucking with that psycho to be with you, and you have me hiding in the room like you're scared of his ass or something." He raised his eyebrow at me.

"Imagine having to kill Crimson to keep me safe, would you want me to hide?"

The question he asked me hit home. All my life Crimson and I have been besties, so if the tables were turned, I would put him on top of the roof just so that I wouldn't have to hurt her. I understood what he was saying now. I also wouldn't tell him anything about her that could hurt her reputation either.

"I give you my word. I will not say anything to anyone, including Crimson." Major took a deep breath waiting about five minutes before he spoke.

"Rush has multiple personalities. This has been going on since we were kids. Killa is the dominant and more aggressive one. He's manipulative and can care less about anyone that crosses his path except for Quinton, me, and now you. I think when you first met him, it was more than likely Rush that you encountered. Somewhere along the line, Killa stepped in and began to care about you. I think he's surfacing more because Rush suffers from schizophrenia as well. All and all he's a hand full and you have to be cautious. He would never hurt Quinton or me, but I'm not sure what would happen if he saw us together like this.

He got up off the floor holding his hand out to help me up. It wasn't really much I could say about the situation, all I could do was be more aware of my surroundings and try to stay off the grid until Major did something about Rush.

FIFTEEN

Crimson

It had been a minute since I saw my father. Although he has been a complete butthole, I had been with him my entire life. I wasn't ashamed to say I missed him, but I just couldn't get with his attitude about me growing into my own. Even though we were going through it, I decided to pay him a visit at the church.

I pulled up to the church, missing everything about being here. This was literally my home away from home. I couldn't wait to see my church families' faces and hug them all. I took a couple of more minutes to collect myself by taking a deep breath. I opened the door to the Range Rover. Getting out, I smoothed my hands over my ivory skirt suit. Once my nude Manolo Blahnik stilettos hit the pavement, I began to get a little nervous. Everyone would be looking because of what I had on. It was totally different than what they have seen me in. My skirt came down mid-thigh, and the matching blazer came to my navel, the nude tank top under it covered my stomach, but the skirt was considerably shorter than what I would normally wear.

I took a deep breath walking into the door. My father's voice boomed through the speakers as he stood in the pulpit on the microphone. I respectfully sat in the back of the church instead of walking to my regular seat in the front. To be honest, I had changed so much that I felt like I didn't deserve that seat anymore.

My father stopped speaking mid-sentence when someone pointed me out to him.

"I see my prodigal child has returned." The church went up with amen, hallelujah, and praise God. I felt my face flush with embarrassment.

"You know the bible teaches us to forgive those who have gone against us and the way of God."

Once my father said that I knew he thought that I had left Quinton. That would never happen, but I decided to suppress my expressions. All I wanted to do was to see my father and see if I could at least get on a level that we could begin to rebuild our broken relationship. I listened attentively as my father spoke to the congregation about forgiving just as God does for us every day and prayed that he would take in his own teachings.

Once the church service was over, I sat in my seat waiting for the members of the church to speak with my dad like they did every Sunday when one of the teens walked up to me.

"Dang Crimson, if going with a dude in the streets is treating you like that, I need to find me one."

I sat bewildered at the fact that she knew my business. That only means that my dad has been talking, and the new me was ready to go in on this little girl. I held my tongue and decided to educate her. Quinton was in a league of his own, and with her way of thinking, she would be the next Keyionte'. Keyionte' has her stuff together now and Major is good for her, but this little chick here would end up running into a Rush Jr. thinking she knows the game and jumping on the first dude that flashed some money in her face.

"Have a seat and let me enlighten you on something lil bihh… I mean little girl." I had to catch myself, and only because I was sitting in my father's church.

"Your man is keeping you in nice clothes, and I saw you when you got out of that Range too. You are doing it out here."

I rolled my eyes. People were always looking at the outside of a situation. Me having all the stuff that Quinton got for me had cost me my father. True, my dad could've gone about things in another way besides what he had decided on, but I could've just been upfront with my dad in the first place and just let everything fall into place. Either way, to be happy with the man I love, I had to give up the man that I thought I knew inside and out. Like I said before, I would have chosen Quinton no matter what.

"Everything you think I have has come at a cost. I won't tell you that I wouldn't make this choice again because I would. I didn't just go out and say I'm looking for a guy that's in the streets with money. My man fell in my lap. He has been good to me, and we love each other. What I really want you to know is just because this worked for me, doesn't mean that it is this way for everyone. I have been gone a little over six months and have seen what fucking with… I mean messing with the wrong man can do to a girl. Don't look at me and want what I have. Always want better for yourself. I know that you can find it."

As she listened to me, I could see the shock in her eyes from the way that I was speaking to her. The people in this church hadn't ever heard me speak using slang my entire life. I could tell she was thinking about the knowledge I had dropped on her. I bet Keyionte' wished she had someone to tell her things like this before she got with Rush. Little info like this could've saved her a lot of time and heartache.

"Thanks for talking to me and I will keep what you said in mind." She got up walking away. If I didn't get anything else out of coming here today, at least I might have saved that girl.

I realized the church had cleared out and made my way to my father's office. I gave a polite knock on the door waiting for him to tell me to come in.

"Come in," I opened the door and before I could say hello he went into his spiel.

"I knew that street urchin wouldn't last that long and you would be back. There's no apology needed for you going against me. I knew it would happen at some point and time. You have practically been the perfect daughter you're entire life. I'm glad you're home, and we have no time to waste you have to get ready for your engagement to our youth pastor, Timothy."

I had heard enough of this. Quinton had told me that something like this would happen.

"I didn't come here because I left Quinton." I was still standing in the doorway. He hadn't given me a chance to get into the office.

"Then why did you come?" His face had twisted with disgust.

That knocked the air out of me. As much as I didn't want to think my dad could be this cold-hearted to his only child, I was wrong. I thought time would do the trick for us, but unfortunately, I was wrong, and I was paying for it with my heart breaking yet again.

"It amazes me that you can stand out there and tell people to forgive and you can't. I'm standing here trying to get back on good terms with you, and all you can do is try to control me. Daddy, I love you, but I love me more. You need to know that Quinton isn't going anywhere. I'm going to leave, but I'm going to leave the door open for you. Once you get in your head that this is my life and I'm going to live it the way I want to, you will be better off.

Before you open your mouth to decline me know that I plan on having kids, and I want you to be able to be a part of their lives, especially since you're the only grandparent that they will have."

I didn't wait for him to say anything before I turned on my thousand-dollar heels walking away. I refused to cry anywhere outside, including my car. I'm far from the weak female I was before I started dating Quinton.

My eyes began to tear up as soon as I got in the driver seat, so I took a couple of deep breaths. I took my feelings and tucked them deep inside myself. I wouldn't let him hurt me again even if he was my father.

I pulled up to the house that Quinton and I now shared soon after. Getting out, Quinton looked at me when I entered the door and followed me to the bedroom. I stripped out of my clothes and got in bed. I didn't want to hear him saying I told you so. To my surprise, he didn't say a word. He just got in the bed next to me pulling me close. I blinked back the tears that I commanded not to drop, closed my eyes, and went into a deep sleep. When I woke up, I hoped that I would be okay. I wouldn't let this consume me with depression. I would get up later knowing that tomorrow would bring me a new day.

I woke in the middle of the night to Quinton staring at me.

"I know he's your father, but all you have to do is say the word, and I will take care of it for you. He will never be able to make you feel this way again. To be honest, the only reason he's still here now is because of you." He moved my hair out of my face so that I could see him. He was dead serious. Damn, I wasn't sure if this made me love him more because he was willing to kill for me, or if I should be cautious because he was ready to kill my father.

"Don't kill my father, Quinton," I told him sternly.

"I won't let another nigga hurt you regardless if he's your daddy or not." My heart expanded listening to my thug in shining armor.

"I feel you babe but let me handle my dad."

I wiggled out of his grasp. Pulling his dick out of his boxers, it hardened in my hand. He knew what was coming next, and I didn't let him down when I wrapped my lips around him. I knew dick wouldn't solve my problems, but coming on his pole would make me feel so much better.

SIXTEEN

Quinton

"Crimson is going to beat your ass when she finds out about this." Major laughed at his own sentence. I smirked a little because him and Keyionte' were going to stop coming at my baby about her fighting skills.

"She will be okay," I told him as I parked in the lot of the church, and we both got out.

I went to the side door that I had seen Crimson come out of some time ago, and to my surprise, it was open. We both stepped in, and an older lady was sitting at the desk. She took one look at us from head to toe and began to yell.

"Pastor!"

We both looked at each other and laughed. You could see the nervousness in her eyes as she appraised Major and I as if we were about to shoot up the office. She began to shuffle papers around the desk pretending to stay busy as she looked at us with a side eye.

"Who would think that walking in here could cause such a commotion? I thought the bible said come as you are," Major stated with a smirk on his face.

"It's only that way if you don't look like us," I told him seriously.

Major took in both of our attire, which was pretty casual. It wasn't like we had on wife beaters and Timberlands. This lady was just tweaking hard. I understand that Chicago can be a dangerous place but damn.

"Mary, why are you screaming like you're crazy?"

I waited for him to look up in my direction, and when he did, I could see the heat in his eyes. Personally, I didn't give a fuck. I would shoot this bitch and him if I had to. I would have to find a way to make it up to Crimson, but she would be good.

"What the hell are you doing here?" he asked both Major and I laughed at the facial expression of the receptionist.

"We need to talk in private," I told him, staring him in the eyes.

"Whatever you have to say to me, you can say it right here."

I cocked my head at the man. If he wanted it this way, then he would have it. I want to keep things between us, and I knew he wouldn't be too happy to see me. Hell, if he wanted me to air his shit out in front of this lady, then so be it. I'm sure Mary would get more than enough to gossip about to his entire church, and I would be fine with that.

"I understand that you don't like me, and I couldn't really give a damn if you do or don't. Personally, I don't like you either. We have one person in common, and that's Crimson. I love her, she loves me, and nothing will change that. So, I don't understand why you consistently want to outcast her when she wants to mend you guys' relationship."

The receptionist's head went from me to Joel waiting for him to respond, while I took in his demeanor wondering what he would say next.

"My Relationship with MY daughter has nothing to do with you. You can leave now!" He turned his back to walk away from me. Everything in me wanted to beat his ass for the disrespect, but I held my composure. My grandmother told me never to disrespect the Lord's house, and that was the only reason I hadn't tore this motherfucker up. Crimson asked me not to kill her father, but she hadn't said anything about whipping his ass though, and this nigga was begging for me to lay hands on him.

"I'll overlook your disrespectful ass for the sake of my woman, but when I tell you this is the last time you will be doing that shit it is." The receptionist jumped up out of her seat looking like she was about to have a heart attack.

"You can't speak like that! Do you know where you're at?" She covered her chest with her hand while her expression reprimanded me.

"I know exactly where I am, and that's probably the only reason both of you aren't dead right now. I'm saying this with all the respect I can muster up. Sit your old ass down before I have my brother do it for you." She quickly sat down.

I took my eyes off her and placed them on Crimson's dad.

"Now, everything concerning Crimson has to do with me. She came here yesterday to make amends and try to get over this bump in the road that you have caused. As much as you want to blame all of this on me, it's not my fault. You were the one that pushed her away from you with your antics of making her choose between you and me. You were the one that made a bogus ass report to get me locked up, and it was you that tried to force her into a marriage with your gay youth minister. This has nothing to do with me. It's all about you trying to control a grown ass woman. While you're here playing the great pillar of the community and pastor, keep this in mind. You were so quick to throw your child away for deciding to live her life for herself, and she's the only reason that you're still breathing."

I have never been the type to get excited about seeing fear in a person's eyes, but seeing the expression in his eyes did something to me. This man had crossed too many lines with me. If I couldn't get the satisfaction of putting a bullet through his skull, I might as well put the fear of God in him. Major and I turned to walk out of the door. There was no need to say anything else.

"You know if you want to keep your word to Crimson, I can make her father a memory for you," Major stated seriously.

I was damn near willing to take him up on his offer, but I couldn't see my girl hurt like that. I don't know what it was, but she had a real nigga soft as hell on her. If my workers found out that I let her dad get away with so much disrespect, they would challenge me in every way possible.

We got back to the hood in record time. I was hungry as hell and pulled over to the restaurant. Before I could get out of the truck, my phone was ringing.

"You know her dad told on you, right?" Major smirked at me.

"That nigga hasn't called her in months. Her daddy calling to snitch about a meeting with her boyfriend would be some bullshit.

"Hey, babe," I finally answered.

"Where are you?" I ran down my location, got out of the car, and ordered my food.

The last thing in the world I expected was for Crimson to pull up outside the restaurant like a bat out of hell. Of all people to be standing in front of me at the time, it just so happen to be the chick Kesha that beat her up at the kickback. Crimson had a fire in her eyes that I had never seen before, and I knew it was about to be some shit. I just wasn't sure why. She stalked up to us, and Kesha moved closer to me.

"You might want to leave now," Major told her with a serious expression on his face.

"What you about to fight for her again? I'm not worried about that bitch," Kesha retorted. I pushed her away from me a little.

"Don't get the bitch out of your face now." Crimson walked up on a smiling Kesha and punched her so fast that I didn't see the connection.

I was so shocked I didn't make a move to break up the fight that was right in front of me. I stood there admiring my girl dragging the bitch down the street. The killing part is this is the classiest way I've ever seen a motherfucker fight. Crimson was out here with a pair of heels on boxing like she was in the ring.

"Beat that bitch's ass!" Major yelled at Crimson while he enthusiastically watched.

Once she was done, Crimson turned to me breathing hard, and I could tell she was still mad. She walked up to me and smacked the shit out of me. Before I knew it, I had her by her neck and slammed against the brick wall.

"You have lost your damn mind? Don't ever put your fucking hands on me!"

I held her up against the wall applying a little pressure to her neck. Crimson thought that because beating women wasn't my specialty, I wouldn't put my hands on her. She had me fucked up though. I was raised that if a person passes a lick, they take one. I felt choking her ass was the better option that way she can't say I beat her up out here.

"Let her go, G." At the sound of Confessa's lethal voice, I dropped her to her feet. She and I had held each other's gaze for a minute.

"Don't ever in your life disrespect me again."

I thought I would see fear in her eyes or sadness, but nope, this girl was pissed off. I guess she could call it even then because I was just as pissed off at her.

"Don't bring your ass back to my house Quinton, or it's going to be some shit." Crimson walked off to her truck burning rubber pulling off.

"You know she's mad. Nigga, she put you out of your own shit." Major laughed while digging through his bag of French fries putting a fork full into his mouth.

"Shut the fuck up before I put bullet holes in your car." Major continued to laugh like I hadn't said anything to him.

I turned around to see my nigga Confessa standing in front of me with something that resembled a smirk on his face. That was saying something about him since the only time I have seen him with half of a smile is when he's torturing someone. His name was Confessa for a reason. The man was deranged and had a certain way to get information out of people. As fucked up as Tan was, he didn't have shit on C. Confessa is in a league of his own. He can get a confession out of a person in five minutes or less.

"You might want to listen to her and not go to the house tonight. She might shoot at you. I know that look in her eyes. When Jinx eyes me like that, I go to my cave."

I nodded my head at him, but Crimson was far from being Jinx or Blaze for that matter. Those women had come up in this hood and moved drugs from Chicago to Texas. Confessa and his best friend Rio stood by them while doing it, but those women were in a class and league of their own.

"She's not about to put me out my own house. If she were like Jinx, I wouldn't think about going home, but she's not." Confessa gave off what I considered a laugh, and that was saying a lot since he was a man of little emotion.

"Is she not a woman?" he asked rhetorically. I thought about his question for a second.

"What brings you out here?" I asked changing the subject.

Confessa, Jinx, Blaze, and Rio had moved out of the hood damn near ten years ago. Nothing was random about him walking through here. He was the type that didn't make a move without a purpose. Although he was in front of me by himself, I knew he wasn't alone. I let my eyes roam to the entire block trying to figure out where Rio or Jinx was hiding.

"Have you talked to Rush lately?" All of the humor was gone from his voice.

"Not for real, we speak during passing. He's been going through something." Rush was trying to find his way, and I had to let him.

"You might want to have a sit-down with him. He's been fucking with the wrong person's daughter. We both know he's a little confused in the head, but he if he beats the daughter of the Italian mob's ass, you will have more problems than you bargain for."

What the fuck was this nigga Rush doing? I knew shit was real because Confessa came to deliver the message personally, and I knew Rush was fucking with Natalia Ferrari.

"Good looking," I told him, trying to wrap my mind around this shit.

Rush was about to get all of us killed. Robert Ferrari didn't play when it came to his daughter, his only child. If Rush fucked this up, Robert wouldn't hesitate to take out my entire family, my team, and their families too. This shit with Rush was getting worse by the minute. Don't get me wrong. I wasn't scared of a motherfucker on this earth. Robert Ferrari was a man just like me. He bleeds just like

I do, but he had something that I didn't, which was a fucking army from Chicago all the way to Italy.

Confessa gave me a nod then turned walking away. Seconds later, I saw Jinx coming from the side of one of the buildings with an M40A5 running to a waiting car. When they drove by, I gave them a nod as they drove by.

"What are we going to do?" Major asked with a serious expression on his face.

"We're finding Rush and are going to dead this shit he has going on with Natalia." I sent him a quick text and then got in my truck. I had business to take care of.

It was now midnight, and I had just pulled up to my house. I was tired as hell looking for Rush and taking care of my trap houses. Rush still hadn't texted me back, and that it was blowing me. All I wanted to do was get in the bed and rub on Crimson's ass until I went to sleep. I hit the garage opener a couple of times, and it wouldn't open.

"What the fuck?"

I shook it a little and hit the button serval times. Finally giving up, I put my truck in park, getting out of the car. I pulled my keys out going through them finding the one for the front door. Placing the key in the door, it wouldn't turn. I jiggled the key in the lock a couple of times.

"Crimson, come open this fucking door." I beat on the door as hard as I could.

"I told you not to bring your butt back to this house," she quickly replied.

She had been sitting at the door waiting for me to come in the house. I could hear her laughing on the other side of the door, and that it had me infuriated. This bitch really put me out my own house, and she thought it was funny. I was going to wrap my hands around her fucking neck once I got in the house.

"Crimson, I'm not about to play with you open this fucking door now."

She started laughing louder as if I was out here doing stand-up comedy. I was too tired for this. She had taken this too far. I stepped back and started kicking the door close to the lock. Her screaming obscenities at me were satisfying. I started hearing the wood cracking under my assault to the door. When I get in this house, I'm going to spank her ass. She wanted to act like a child, so I would treat her like one.

SEVENTEEN

Crimson

This nigga had lost his mind. He was kicking the door off the hinges. The part that was getting to me is that he was mad about me locking him out after all the events that happened today. I had gone to confront him about harassing my father when I caught him with that hood rat ass bitch from the kickback. Then he had the nerve to put his hands on me like I was some random bitch. Had he not done any of that, he wouldn't be kicking in the freaking door like he was crazy.

"I'm a give you one more chance to open this fucking door Crimson or I'm a make me slamming you against that wall seem like a walk in the park!" he yelled through heavy breaths. I moved away from the door.

"Fuck you, Quinton," I told him for the second time today.

I could hear him take a couple of deep breaths then kicked the door three more times before it came crashing down in front of me. I took in his appearance and knew I had messed up royally. The heat in his eyes told me that he was ready to smack me around for sure.

"Why the hell do you want to play with me, Crimson? I have too much shit going on out here in the streets to have to kick down the door at my own fucking house. You are supposed to be my solace during all this shit, but you want to play fucking games!" he yelled as he stalked up to me seeming larger than life. I held my breath as he backed me up into the wall, and I was caught off guard when a fist went past my head into the wall. I dang near jumped out of my skin.

"I swear to God if I hit women, I would fuck you clean the fuck up right now."

From the look in his eyes, I knew he wanted nothing more than to beat my ass. He had a point to make with me, but I had one to make with him too. I wasn't stupid enough to press my luck though. I stood there in front of him silently glaring at him. We had a stare down for a second before he walked away stomping up the stairs.

"Since you wanted to be smart and change the locks stay up and wait for someone to come fix this door!" he yelled before slamming the door to our bedroom.

I went to the living room, grabbing my gun from the end table. Sitting on the couch, I couldn't sit here with my door wide open and not have protection. I was thinking about what Quinton said about having too much going on to be dealing with me. I lay my gun across my lap and picked up my cell phone. Although Quinton trained me to take care of myself, he kept me in the dark about a lot of things that are going on. He didn't feel that I should put myself in things that I couldn't handle. He wasn't wrong. I knew nothing about the drug game besides that he was someone important in these streets. Tae, on the other hand, was able to get more out of Major than I could get out of Quinton. I sent Tae a quick text about meeting up tomorrow so that I could see what was going on. She sent back a thumbs up.

The Next Day

I sat at the Applebee's waiting for Tae to show up. We hadn't been out in a while, and it felt good to get to have some girl time. Since they found out that Rush was practically obsessed with Keyionte', the men usually stayed close to us. Major wasn't playing about her either. With her new crib came a new tinted out car, but the majority of the time, Major or Quinton picked her up from home. I sat sipping my drink looking around for her and smiled when I saw her come through the door.

"Crimson." Her smile was big as she walked up to me. I stood up, and we embraced then sat down.

"I missed you," I told her, taking in her appearance. She looked good and happy. It felt like I hadn't seen her since forever.

"I missed you too," she told me. We sat there silent for a minute.

"Although I miss you, I know this isn't a bitch let's go out and chill type thing. I can tell by your expression that something is wrong with you, so let it out."

I could never hide anything from her. We both knew each other better than we knew ourselves. I took a deep breath and was about to tell her everything, but the server popped up at the table. We both gave our orders. We knew exactly what we wanted to eat because we always ordered the same thing every time we came here.

"I need to ask you a couple of questions," I told her then took a sip of my drink.

"Does it have anything to do with Quinton hemming you up yesterday?" *Dang, Major had told her about that.* You would think with her being my bestie that I would be able to tell her first. I couldn't get mad about what she knew already.

"That too but last night Quinton and I kind of gotten into it once he got home."

I gave her the short version of what happened between Quinton and me, and to say she was shocked was an understatement. The Quinton that I had first met changed on me once he was under pressure. Could I really be mad about that when I had made a complete one-eighty on him? The girl he met the day the car broke down was long gone, but he'd made me who I am now.

"Okay, so you pissed him off. He should've whipped your ass, but he didn't, and now you mad and want to hide at my crib. You know that's the first place he is coming, and he's going to drag you out of the house by all that pretty ass red hair."

I rolled my eyes at her. She had to be crazy if she thought I would go to her house to hide. Going there isn't hiding. Doing that is like texting the nigga telling him where I am.

"Um no, I'm not a dummy. I called you here because you know what goes on in the streets, I don't. I want to know what's going on. Last night Quinton told me that he had too much going on to be dealing with my shit." Keyionte' sat stoically.

"If G didn't tell you, why should I?" I cocked my head at her. She was my day one and was coming at me like I was Quinton's side chick.

"If you don't start talking, we are going to be in here fighting, and you still gone be my main chick afterwards." I tapped my fingers on the table waiting for her to open her mouth.

"I'm going to tell you, but you know that I'm nowhere near scared of you."

"Yeah, yeah, bitch talk," I told her, folding my hands on the table as she gave me an amused expression.

"Yesterday after everything happened with you, some of the trap houses were robbed, and they killed a couple of the workers. On top of all that, Rush's crazy ass is into some shit that could fuck everyone over if things goes left. When G said he has too much going on, he wasn't lying."

I sat back in my chair thinking about everything that Keyionte' told me. The server walked over to our table placing our food in front of us. The talking ceased as we started separating our food, placing half on each other's plates.

EIGHTEEN

Rush

I sat outside of Applebee's waiting patiently for Keyionte' to come out and lead me to where she lived. I have never had trouble leaving a bitch alone, but for some reason, I couldn't shake Keyionte'. Once I talked to Major, I decided to let her do her, but for some reason, I couldn't. This girl was like a drug to me. I even tried talking to someone else to get over her, but that wasn't going too good though. This bitch was getting on my nerves.

"I thought we were going somewhere special to eat. Why the fuck are we at Applebee's, and why are we sitting in the parking lot?"

I cringed at her Minnie Mouse sounding voice. When I first met her, I thought it was cute, but after a couple of months of hearing her nonstop chatter, I was annoyed by it.

"Can you just shut the fuck up for a minute? I'm surprised your father hasn't whacked you just off the sound of your voice." Her mouth dropped open. She was shocked, but this was the first time she had shut up since I started fucking her.

"I can't believe you just spoke to me like that?" she whined and made me want to punch her in the face.

"I'm dead ass serious. Shut the fuck up before I shut you up."

I looked at the time as she sighed and huffed. My level of anger increased as I thought about the reason that I was sitting next to her in the first place. I had motive behind talking to Natalia. I needed her to get me close to her dad because that man had the best coke in the city since Jinx and Confessa ran the hood. What Quinton was running was the next best. As they say, money talks and bullshit walks, so he was willing to deal, if he was able to take Quinton down. As crazy as it may seem, he didn't want our territory. He just wanted the money that Quinton was making now. I gave him what he wanted, but the bad part about it was that I had to keep his daughter satisfied until I got what I wanted.

"My father is going to hear about how you're treating me." I closed my eyes to keep from punching her.

"What your father will be happy about is not hearing your voice again. If you ever threaten me, I'm going to cut your fucking tongue out of your mouth." She quickly snapped her mouth close rolling her eyes at me. I see her father didn't raise a fool.

"Let me know if the girl with the red hair comes out of there," I told Natalia, laying my head on the headrest and closing my eyes just for a minute.

Knowing I had found Keyionte' I could relax just a little. I felt myself getting excited about being able to get back with my baby, I knew I had fucked up, but that was months ago. After all this time, I know she forgave me and was ready for daddy to step back in and take care of her. I opened my eyes a little, but not enough to let Natalia know that I was watching the door too.

After a couple of hours of waiting in the parking lot, I had finally gotten what I wanted. Keyionte' and I both were pulling up to her house. I parked across the street from her and waited until she was halfway up her walkway before opening the door to my car.

"Don't get out of this car, or I'ma fuck you clean up," I told Natalia before closing the door doing a half walk/ half run catching up to Keyionte' right before she closed the door. I stuck my foot in the door holding it open.

"What the fuck?" Keyionte' yelled, putting her weight against the door trying to push it close on me. It was nothing her small frame could do to keep me out of the house.

"Get off the door before you make me mad," I raised my voice at her to let her know I wasn't playing.

At the sound of my voice,I could tell she froze because she stopped putting force on the door. I opened the door, and when I looked into her face, all I saw was fear in her eyes. I took in the layout of her townhouse and was impressed. She has done her thing in here. The set up included a cream leather furniture accented with purple throw pillows, a seventy-inch television, a cream throw rug with different shades of purple and gray, and a glass table and end table set. I can see living by herself had her coming into her own person. This little set up was cute, but all this girly shit would have to change once I moved in.

"What are you doing here?" she had finally found her voice. I raised a questioning brow at her.

"Fuck you mean what am I doing here? You are the wrong one asking the questions. How about you tell me why you've been hiding from a nigga like I just did you so wrong?"

She swallowed hard looking at me like she was trying to figure me out.

"TALK!" I yelled at her, causing her to jump and take a couple of steps away from me.

I was trying to do this the easy way, but she was going to make me fuck her up in this house. *It's a damn shame that this bitch just won't let me love her.*

Keyionte'

I stood in my house shaking in fear because my worst nightmare had come true. The devil was standing at my threshold.

"TALK!" Rush or should I say Killa yelled at me, and I swear I felt my bladder about to release all the drinks that I had tonight.

I knew the day would come that I would have to face him. I just didn't know it would be today. He was standing in front of me acting like that night never happened like he was gone on a long vacation and I had been home missing him. He wanted me to welcome his crazy ass back into my life with open arms and kisses, but I couldn't, and I was scared out of my mind of what he would do to me.

"You raped me," I said in a voice that I didn't recognize as my own.

"Rape? The fuck you mean, Keyionte'? I can't take what's already mine," he told me with a cold stare.

As much as I wanted to cower and look down at the floor, I couldn't because I wasn't sure of what he would do to me. Instead of becoming a victim to him, I took another step away from him.

"The shit you did to me that night was foul as hell Rush, and you know it. Not only did you fuck me over, but you also embarrassed me in front of our friends. You violated me." My voice became stronger as anger took over me. Instead of me shaking from fear of him, I was vibrating from the anger that was consuming me.

"Those are your friends, not mine. My friends would've never come between what you and I have. It's cool though. I'm back, and I will never leave you again. You and I will live together and will die together."

He smiled a smile that didn't reach his eyes. This motherfucker was off his rocker for real. He might as well tell me that he was going to put a bullet in my head.

My phone started ringing, and I knew it was Crimson calling to make sure I made it in. I didn't even attempt to answer the phone. I wasn't sure what he would do if I did.

"You're not going to get that?" he asked. I shook my head no. The phone stopped ringing and started right back.

"It might be important," he told me acting concerned. I turned my head quizzically at him.

"How did you find me?" I asked he smirked at me and the phone began to ring again.

"I knew Crimson was going to lead me right to you. You two can't stay away from each other too long."

Although I was mad about his presence, he was smart with that move. My phone started ringing for the fourth time, and I figured this time it was Major. They would be here in no time.

"Answer that damn phone!"

Once the phone rang again, I didn't even look at the screen. I just swiped my finger across accept.

"Hey, yeah, I'm okay. I accidentally left my phone on top of the car in the garage," I smoothly told Major gave him a couple of yes, and no answers then hung up.

Turning my back to Rush, I casually walked to the couch sitting down, only for someone to bang on my door like the law.

"Open this door, Rush," someone said in a voice like Minnie Mouse.

I raised my eyebrow at him. This nigga was so busy following me, and a bitch was following him. How ironic? I got up walking to the door, but Rush swung it open before I could get to it. A petite, beautiful woman stepped in the door.

"I thought I told you to stay the hell in the car?" Rush yelled at her. Unfazed she stepped around him looking me up and down.

"Who is this?" She looked around Rush staring at me like they weren't uninvited guests in my shit. Her voice was irritating, and I wanted to snatch her damn voice box out.

"Bitch, I'm nobody. Take your man out of my house and leave," I told her.

"This is my bitch," Rush said seriously, pointing at me.

"No, you have to be wrong because last time I checked, I am your girl and I don't do that sister wife shit, so there's no need for us to be here," she told him pulling at his arm to walk out the door.

"Bitch, you can go, but I'm staying here," Rush retorted.

"My father is going to kill you and your bitch," she told him about to walk out the door. Rush pulled his gun out pointing it at the woman and shot her.

"Bitch, didn't I tell you don't threaten me with your father again?"

My mouth dropped at how easy he was able to pull the trigger on this woman. I didn't know who the hell her father was, but that was definitely Rush's ass on a platter, and I couldn't have been happier about his future demise. *I wonder if once he is killed the other people living in him will die too.* A smile touched my lips at my own thoughts.

"See this shit, baby? She thought she was going to have us killed, now look at her."

"You think shooting this woman makes all this better. You have more than likely made things a whole lot harder." I walked over to the woman lying at my front door and checked to see if she was still alive.

"What are you tripping for, baby? I did this for us. Now, do you see how much I love you? I just killed this bitch so that we can survive."

I kept my hand on the woman's stomach to keep her from bleeding out so much. This man was crazy for real, and I couldn't figure out why I was with him in the first place. Rush moved over to me grabbing me by the arm trying to pick me up off the floor. I dropped my weight down to make him have to put more strength into getting me off the floor. I went into my pocket pulling my knife out and took it across his face and arm. He had a look of shock on his face, but once he realized what I had done, he smacked me so hard I slid across the floor.

Rush stalked over to me getting blood everywhere in his path. I knew he was about to beat the hell out of me. We both heard someone burning rubber on the corner at the same time. I knew it was Major and G, but he must have known too because he turned running out the door. I said a silent prayer thanking God for being on time. Major and G rushed the door. Major came right over to me while G stood in the doorway looking down at the woman bleeding on my floor.

"Damn!" he exploded.

NINETEEN

Quinton

I stood frozen in place as I saw Natalia Ferrari lying on the floor in a pool of her own blood. It was about to be some shit, and we weren't equipped enough for war. I bent down checking her vitals, and she was still alive. I picked her up quickly knowing that I could get her to the hospital quicker than waiting for the paramedics. I didn't have to tell Major and Keyionte' to come on because they were right on my heels. I placed Natalia in the back seat of the truck and then hopped back there with her. Major got behind the wheel of the car peeling off before the driver door was closed.

"Call Crimson and tell her don't open the door or leave out the house until the man that was at the restaurant the other day gets there."

Keyionte' pulled out her phone doing as I told her, and all you could hear was Crimson mouth moving a mile a minute with question after question. I pulled the phone from Keyionte'.

"Do what I told you to do. I don't have time for this shit, Crimson." I hung the phone up, tossing it back to Keyionte'. I really have to get Crimson's ass under control. Shit is about to get really hot around here, and I can't have her getting herself killed.

"You know what we have to do now?" Major was looking in the rearview mirror at me.

I nodded my head looking down at the innocent woman laying across the back seat bleeding to death. I had let Rush get away with too much. I should've sent him to counseling or the nuthouse a long time ago. He had been a loose cannon for a long ass time now. On top of all the shit happening in the streets, now I have to deal with this. Major pulled up to the hospital doors in no time. I picked Natalia up and ran inside the emergency room doors.

"Can someone help her please?" I placed her on a gurney watching them rush her behind the double doors. I pulled my phone out of my pocket calling Confessa.

"Rush done fucked up and shot Natalia. Can you go to my house and get my girl for me? I can't lose her to this bullshit, man."

I knew what it was from here on out. To some of the niggas sitting in the waiting room, I sounded like a bitch. Real talk though, coming from nothing and gaining all of Humboldt Park, I knew that my most prize position was the woman that I would live and die for. These mob motherfuckers will take everything and everyone in sight out if they felt like they were being crossed. The truth of all this is that Rush had crossed the invisible line and was going to take all of us down with him. I didn't have anything to do with it, but I was guilty by association. There is going to be a war, and I'm right in the middle of the motherfucker.

"I'll send Jinx and Blaze for your girl. You have bigger problems. Meet me at the main house." I listened to everything Confessa was telling me.

"What the fuck?" This night was becoming worse by the second. "We out," I told Major, walking out the doors we had just walked into. I hope Natalia survive. I would have to check back on that because right now I have to get to my trap.

"What's up, G? Talk to me."

I looked in the back seat at Keyionte' thoughtfully before I said anything. I quickly realized that whatever I said didn't matter because she was stuck with us for now just like Crimson.

"Confessa and Rio caught some niggas robbing the main house."

"I guess this is our lucky night, huh?" Major replied with a sarcastic expression on his face. I ran everything that Confessa had told me down to Major.

"We need to drop Keyionte' off with Crimson."

I diverted my eyes to her before turning them back on the road.

"She's coming with us Jinx and Blaze are going to meet us there with Crimson," I told him going around a driver that was going so slow we might as well had been on pause.

I drove like a bat out of hell getting to the trap, couldn't wait to find out who had the audacity to test God. I pulled up to the house burning rubber, stopping directly in at the front door.

Walking into the house, I laughed at the sight before me. Confessa and Rio had everyone sitting with their backs against the wall Indian style. All of them had a look of terror in their eyes, and I knew Confessa had done some crazy shit. None of them were tied or taped up, yet they all sat there like obedient children.

"It took you long enough," Confessa said, keeping his eyes on a man in front of him.

"It's only been ten minutes, old man."

He made a sound that I took as a fuck me and continued to stare down the man that he had tied to the chair. He finally turned to look at me.

"He's all yours. Make me proud."

I took off my jacket, stepping to the man sitting in the chair acting like he owns everything and everyone in here. Rolling up my sleeves, I knew it was time to put in work. Motherfuckers were definitely going to feel my wrath in this bitch.

TWENTY

Crimson

I quickly grabbed a couple of things. From the urgency in both Keyionte' and Quinton's voices, I figured I wouldn't be back home for a couple of days. I wasn't sure of everything that was going on, but I knew it had something to do with Rush's nutty behind. Ten minutes after the call, someone was ringing the doorbell. I figured it was the guy that Quinton said would come to get me, so I opened the door before realizing the other part of the conversation until I saw two pretty women standing in my doorway.

"Damn," I said aloud thinking this was either about to be some bullshit about Quinton or Rush had paid a couple of bad bitches to pull an abduction. The way these women was dressed, my neighbors would think that I was about to go out for the night. No one would ever think to question two older females dressed to kill in stilettos.

"Who are you?" I asked, blocking their way into the house.

"It's a fine time to ask, especially since you've already opened the door," the darker of the two said with a smirk on her face.

"Like the door would stop us if we wanted to get in anyway," the lighter one that was nailing me with a stare replied before pushing past me. Both of them walked into my house like they owned it, looking around.

"Nice house," one of them said. Both of them turned around toward me only to stare down the barrel of my Ruger.

"That's cute, but this is what we carry." Before I could blink, these bitches had four guns pointed at me.

"Put your gun down before you hurt yourself," the light-skinned chick said.

I stood there staring them down and didn't drop my gun. Yeah, they had four guns to my one, but if I needed to, I could shoot one of them.

"You two first," I replied, aiming my gun at the lighter of the two. Since she was doing all the talking, I would feel better shooting her.

We were at a standoff, and neither of us was about to drop our guns. I was having a stare down with the lighter one, so I hadn't paid attention to the darker one moving until she was right beside me doing some type of move snatching my gun from me. It was then that I knew I was jacked.

"We're not about to play with you. You're going to do exactly what we say, or you won't make it to your next destination," the darker one told me.

I should kick my own ass for being stupid as hell. I felt tears prickle in the back of my eyes, but I refuse to let these bitches see me break down. Whatever my fate is, I will take it like a woman. I grabbed my bag and willingly walked out the door.

Sitting blindfolded and nervous in the second row of a Suburban with heavily tinted windows, I wasn't sure what was about to happen to me. All I knew is that the darker of the two girls had a gun pointed at the back of my head. I knew if they wanted me dead, I would have been by now, but at this point, I wasn't certain that it was Rush that had me abducted. I recalled the conversation that

Keyionte' and I had at the restaurant and knew that someone had been sticking up Quinton's trap houses. Someone wanted him out of the game and fast. I was beginning to think that I had become collateral. I sent up a silent prayer hoping that Quinton would find me before I was killed. Maybe they would call him and demand something for my safe return. I rolled my eyes behind the blindfold knowing that even if he gave them everything he owned, I still wouldn't make it from this.

About thirty minutes later, we were pulling over. The blindfold was snatched off my eyes, and the light-skinned woman looked me in the eyes.

"This is going to be a smooth transaction. You hear me?" I nodded my head at her.

"If you think about pulling some bullshit, I will put a bullet in your spine, and we won't have to worry about you running away anymore." I nodded my head again.

Getting out of the truck grabbing my bag, one of them walked ahead of me, and one was behind me. We walked up a few stairs into a house. Stepping into the small hallway, I heard someone inside moaning as if they were in pain, and my stomach dropped to my feet.

The light skinned one slowly opened the door stepping inside then gave me a nod to come in behind her, but she was smiling at me like this was some kind of a joke.

"What's up, Jinx?" I heard Major's voice say.

I walked through the house with my mouth hanging open. I looked from corner to corner seeing people sitting on the floor like they were scared to move. In the middle of the living room was my man standing over a white man with a horse bit in his mouth with the leather of it hooked to a piece of metal that was mounted into the wall. His hands and feet were taped to the chair that he was sitting in, and he was missing eight of his fingers. Quinton removed the bit from his mouth.

"Are you ready to talk now?"

Quinton had an air about him that I had never seen before. I guess this is what he meant a while back when he told me about how he was not so forgiving to people.

"Fuck you!" the guy retorted before the bit was shoveled back into his mouth.

"You don't follow instructions well, Crimson. I told you not to let anyone in the house except Confessa."

I flinched. It was as if his tone of voice had smacked me across the face. I didn't know who the dude covered in blood was standing in front of me, but he wasn't my nigga.

"How do you know I didn't do what you said?" I asked him.

He pulled out his phone showing me a picture of myself in the truck blindfolded. The dark-skinned woman had her gun to my head with a huge smile on her face. I wanted to roll my eyes at him, but I knew not to push him any further than he had been pushed for the day. I had brought all this on myself, and I could admit that, but not in front of everyone in this room. The dude Confessa had what resembled a smirk on his face. I wanted to lash out at someone, but I knew it wouldn't be him because he scared the mess out of me just by breathing.

I did the next best thing. I stood in the corner next to Keyionte' and didn't say a word to anyone.

"Crimson, meet your captors Jinx and Blaze." Major pointed to the light-skinned woman then the darker one. They both smiled at me.

"Sorry we had to do that to you, but we couldn't resist it," Blaze said still smiling like this was a joke. I rolled my eyes then moved closer to Keyionte' so that we could talk.

"G, you will never get what you need out of him. Let me at him," Confessa told Quinton while pulling what looked like a thin blade.

Quinton moved out of the way letting Confessa take his place in the middle of the floor. Confessa gave the man a smile that didn't reach his eyes. It caused a chill down my spine, and every piece of hair on my body stood up.

"You know what this is?"

The man in the chair eyes got wide with fear, and my stomach began to churn. I had no idea what he was about to do but from the blade in his hand and the look in his eyes I knew it was going to be brutal. Confessa took the blade so lightly cross the man's wrist, and I didn't know he had cut him until he took out a vice grip looking tool and pulled the man's skin back up his arm. He was skinning him alive. Once he was done with his left arm up to his elbow, he pulled out a bottle of ammonia pouring some on him. The man wiggled in the chair and screamed the entire time that it took Confessa to do all of this.

"You know what's next. Jinx, get his pants off and make sure he's not able to use that motherfucker again." Jinx walked over to Confessa and kicked the man over, and he screamed.

I began to feel dizzy, and my stomach turned. I covered my mouth running through the house pushing doors open trying to find the bathroom. When I felt I couldn't hold it in any longer, I found the bathroom just in time losing the contents of my stomach. Quinton was on my heels in the bathroom hovering over me. He rubbed my back soothingly until I got myself together. He wet a paper towel and began to wipe my face. I moved out of his reach.

"I got it."

Looking everywhere else except his face, I didn't want him to touch me as my mind flashed back to what he had done to that man. He gave me a perplexed look taking a small step back then continued wiping my face like I hadn't said a word to him. The man that was in here wiping my face with a wet paper towel wasn't the man that had stood in the middle of the floor about fifteen minutes ago.

"I can't do this, Quinton. I thought I could, but I can't be a part of this."

His hand stopped moving, and he stared at me like I was a stranger. I could see his mind working overtime as the impact of my words hit him. He went back to taking care of me, but as he did, he searched my eyes. Quinton was a thinker, and I knew he was going over the possibilities of me leaving him in his head as he was silent. The man that was making sure I was okay at this moment was the man that I knew and loved.

"Is that what you really want, Crimson?" Quinton asked me while sitting me in his lap.

I put my head in the crook of his neck and nodded my head yes. We sat there for a minute before I got up and walked out of the bathroom, stepping into another room until Keyionte' walked in telling me it was time to go.

TWENTY-ONE

Quinton

"Nigga, I knew Confessa was crazy, but damn, did he have to do all that and set the fucking house on fire?"

I laughed at Major. He was dead ass serious, but that's how Confessa got down. He obtained the information that we needed and only eight people walked out of the house alive before he set it on fire. We weren't even able to get the money and drugs. It had gone up in flames too. I wasn't worried about it. Confessa and Jinx would replace what I lost, but to see half a million dollars' worth of product and money get destroyed was fucked up.

"You know he has his way of doing things, and we asked for help. We will all work together. We put the fear of God in motherfuckers, but it's nothing like how niggas fear Confessa."

Major nodded his head in understanding. Confessa, Jinx, Blaze, and Rio were in a class of their own. I've seen men in high places shake in their presence. When they were in the drug game, their reach was across the United States and went over to Japan once Rio's mother came back into the picture. They were the only people that I know that retired without one of them losing their lives.

We rode in silence for a minute both of us in our thoughts probably thinking about what dude had told us after Jinx peeled and sliced his dick off. I cringed at the thought. Rush had made a deal with the mob so that he could take everything I have. He didn't know that at the end of everything, they were going to kill him too. I couldn't believe he was so quick to destroy everything we worked so hard for. When I ate, that nigga ate too. Too much had gone down within the last twenty-four hours. My best friend had crossed me, and my girl had dumped me.

"Crimson told me she wanted to leave me." Major turned to me, his expression serious.

"What did you tell her?" I exhaled loudly.

"I told her when this is over she could go, but I'm not letting her go nowhere, bro."

Out of all the chicks I've have been with none of them can compare to her. I would tie her ass up in the basement and won't let her out of there until she changed her mind.

I checked my rearview mirror for the third time. Seeing the same car behind me, I made a quick right turn, and the car turned with me. I hit a few blocks watching the car follow me turn for turn. I made a couple of calls and then led them right where I wanted them. The location where I wanted them must've been where they wanted my ass too because three more cars came and blocked me off. Six men got out of their cars, placing FNP 90s submachine guns in our faces. Major and I both put our hand up. They opened our doors, and we both stepped out of the truck.

"Damn G, we in high demand around this motherfucker. Who knew it took six motherfuckers to roll up on a couple of men like ourselves." Major had a big ass smile on his face until the man closest to him raised his gun to hit him.

"There's no need for that. We're only here to talk." Robert Ferrari stepped out of the Black truck he was in looking like he was about to step onto the red carpet. Major and I both dropped our hands.

"You know I'm going to kill him, right?" Major told him as we stepped closer to Robert. Robert smiled at us like we were old time friends.

"Just tell me where Rush is," Robert demanded.

"Shit, if we knew that you would have to stand in line because we're fucking him up first," Major stated.

"What I want to know is how do you lose the man that you made a deal with to take over my territory, and he's the same man that was fucking and shot your daughter? I think it's so funny that I've never done a thing to you. I have never stepped on your toes in any way, but you want to take me out because a crazy motherfucker told you to." I watched his demeanor chance from arrogant to pissed off in seconds.

"You have me mistaken. I take orders from no one," Robert replied angrily as his face turned beet red.

"You have me mistaken as well, Robert. You pull up on me with these motherfuckers pointing their guns in my face like I'm not a fucking God in these streets. I'm the nigga that should be standing in front of you demanding shit since you decided to take my drugs and my fucking money. Even after finding out all of that, I decided to let your daughter live. I was the one that made sure she stayed alive to tell you what happened to her. I could've sent one of my nurses into her room to put a fucking air bubble in her IV after you left this morning."

Robert took a step back after I told him that. I know this nigga didn't think I made it this far being a fucking dummy and not knowing what was going on.

"Maybe we can come to an agreement?" I cocked my head at him.

"Says the man that shook hands with the devil," I retorted. This man had me fucked up and pissed off. On the inside, I was about to explode, but on the outside, I looked calm as hell.

"We can make this work, or I could take everyone you love." I laughed at him. He really had no idea that I was smarter than I looked.

"You need to look around you. I could end every one of you right now. Even your daughter isn't safe. Her guard outside her door is taking a nice nap right now, and a nurse is right at her side ready to make her take a dirt nap."

Robert looked around seeing red dots on all six of his men

heads. Major walked over to us showing him a picture of his daughter with a nurse standing next to her bed with a needle in her IV line. Then a red dot appeared over his heart and moved slowly to his head. I smiled at him.

"Killing me will cause a war that you will not win." He stood in front of me calm as can be, but I could see the fear in his eyes.

"You might be right, but you nor your bloodline won't be here to see it. Tell your men to drop their guns, and we can talk about this like civilized men."

As the last word left my mouth, he nodded his head for his men to drop their guns. The red dots never moved from any of them as he gave me a cocky smile and nodded his head at his men to lower their weapons.

"I'll tell you what," he said with a thick Italian accent, then stopped thoughtfully.

"I can forget all of this, and I will even give you back everything that was taken from you. All you have to do is take care of a little problem that we both have. I don't have to tell you what or who it is," he said smugly.

He really did think he had the upper hand, even with a high-powered rifle aimed at his head.

"Well, I really can't forget about the fact that you and my right hand tried to fuck me over, but I'll take care of the problem personally. We are done here but let me leave you with a bit of advice. As much as you would like to think you're untouchable, you're not. Just like Rush got to your daughter, I can too. The mob has an enemy that's more powerful than they are and I just so happen to be friends with them. Watch who you come after because your family might not want to cross the country to help you. Tell Natalia I said get well soon."

I turned my back to him walking back to my truck.

"You know we're not finding Rush until he wants to be found, right?" Major told me once we had closed the doors on the truck. I nodded my head at him while answering.

"Yup, let's get back to the house so we can grab Keyionte' and Crimson."

I was the last one to pull off. I had to make sure any of the Italians weren't following us. The last thing I wanted to do was lead them back to our friend's house and right to our women.

~

When we walked in the door of Confessa and Jinx's mansion, Crimson and Keyionte' were both holding rifles in their hands.

"What the hell are y'all doing with those?" I questioned, snatching the gun out of Crimson's hand. Crimson rolled her eyes at me taking the gun back walking to sit on the couch.

"Why did you teach me to shoot if you weren't going to want me to help you when you needed it?"

Crimson started breaking the gun down like she was a professional sharpshooter. I turned to look at Jinx, Blaze, Rio, and Confessa.

"What the hell have y'all done to them within a couple of hours?" Rio threw his hands up and stepped back while the other three smirked at me before Confessa turned walking away.

"Instead of standing in my living room thinking the worse, you need to thank us for getting your girl back on point, and you need to thank her for her perfect aim. She's the one that kept that beam on Robert while you were talking to him. It's amazing what a woman will do when their man might be about to take a bullet to the head." Jinx turned walking in the direction Confessa had gone. I sat on the couch next to Crimson, pulling her closer to me.

"Thanks for helping me out earlier, baby. When this shit is over, I'll set you up wherever you want to move. You don't have to stay with me, but I'll make sure you're taking care of."

I meant that shit. Crimson pushed me away from her getting up and pacing the floor in front of me. I looked around the room, and everyone had cleared out.

"I know what I said last night, but I can't believe you would let me go just like that." She snapped her fingers. I saw the fiery in her eyes, and that it had me baffled. Women were so fucked up. You tell them, no, and they have an attitude. You give them what they want, and they want to fight you for that.

"I'm confused. What the fuck do you want, Crimson?" She had the nerve to place her hands on her hips that had rounded more since she had been staying with me. She was looking at me like I was an idiot for not reading her mind

"Yesterday was a lot for me to take in. I had never seen anything like that in my life, so I was overwhelmed and bewildered by what was happening right before me. I have only seen things like that in movies, and to see that side of you, just did something to me. If someone else I walked in to see doing cutting off extremities, I might have been able to stomach it more than I did. All I'm trying to say is that I'm sorry for trying to bail on you when you needed me most. It won't happen again, babe." She leaned in kissing my lips.

"Y'all better get a room. Ain't no fucking on my couch. That couch cost me twenty grand!" Jinx yelled from one of the rooms. I laughed.

"Crimson, I know you think that I was going to let you leave, but you weren't going anywhere. I was going to tie you to the bed and wasn't letting you get up until I was sure you were carrying my seed."

She rolled her eyes and laughed like I was playing, but she wouldn't have thought it was a joke when she found herself bound and ass up in my bed.

"Why until I was pregnant?" she quizzed.

"You wouldn't have left knowing you have my child," I told her seriously.

She might have thought I didn't pay attention to her, but I knew she missed her father, and she wouldn't deny me a life with my kid.

"You ready to go to Major's?" I asked her. She nodded her head getting up. As she stood up, I smacked her on the ass watching it jiggle a little.

TWENTY-TWO

Keyionte'

"All that shit she was talking, and she's in there with her tongue down that nigga's throat," Blaze told us as she shook her head at the image.

Blaze, Jinx, and I sat in the room watching Crimson and Quinton on the monitors to see if she was going to play hard to get. Jinx turned the microphone on telling them to get a room. I checked out all the monitors, and you could see almost every inch of their house except for two bedrooms and the sitting room in the basement where the men were. They had their house hooked completely up. You couldn't get into their house without the code to the door. I don't know exactly who would be crazy enough to run in this motherfucker, but they couldn't get in without someone in the house knowing they were here.

"Time to go." Quinton had opened the door to the camera room with a smile on his face like he knew what we were up to as soon as we walked out of the living room.

I grabbed my duffle bag from my overnight stay, and when I walked out of the room, the entire group was waiting at the front door.

"When this is over maybe we can all take a vacation together,"

Blaze insisted. We all agreed. The women gave Crimson, and I hugs as the men shook up.

"Call us if you need us," Rio told the men as we walked out to the Range Rover.

A Week Later

"I'm tired of this freaking house!" Crimson yelled, walking through the house like a mad woman.

We had been on lockdown for over a week, and it didn't seem like we were going to get out any time soon. Major sat on the couch smirking at her before getting up.

"I'm about to take a shower. Handle the brat while I'm upstairs." He walked off as I rolled my eyes at his retreating back.

I waited until I heard the music blasting before I walked over to Crimson grabbing her by the arm and pulled her over to the couch.

"Why do we have to go through this every other day, Crim? You know we can't go out until the lunatic is dead. Unless you want to be a pawn in his twisted ass game, I advise you to calm the fuck down."

Her eyes got big. I knew she was about to go through her normal banter.

"That's easy for you to say. Most of the time my man is the one out in the streets trying to catch the fucking maniac you just had to have. We wouldn't be in this shit if you could just say no and keep your fucking legs closed."

My heart split in two at her words. She had never said anything like this before. Yes, part of this was my fault. I could admit that, but did she have to be so brutal? Rush was a fatal attraction but did she really feel that all of this was my fault. I couldn't control the things that was going on in that man's head. Hell, he couldn't control the shit. I sat there watching Crimson sitting with her arms folded across her chest. She cursed at me and everything, she usually on used that language when things got real.

"Fuck you, Crimson. You have always had this high and fucking mighty air about you. You think that you're the perfect person in this perfect little world your father and Quinton have made for you.

Guess what, you're not. Most of this shit is going on because Rush feel like once you came along, his two best friends pushed him to the side to cater to you. Since you want to play the blame game, blame your fucking self."

I got up walking towards the front door.

"Another thing, if you want to leave, here's the door. Get the fuck out!"

I opened the door looking at Crimson only to see the horror on her face. I slowly turned around and pissed on myself looking into Rush's demented face. I backed away slowly. Crimson and I both screamed at the top of our lungs but were not being heard over the music.

"You thought you could get away without getting what was coming to you, huh?" Rush stepped into the house.

For each foot that I backed away, he was stepping a foot and a half towards me. I bumped into Crimson, and she snaked a hand around my stomach, turning us both, placing him in front of us and our backs toward the door. My heart was beating so fast and hard that it felt like it would beat right out of my chest. I thought of all the times G and Major told us it didn't matter if we were in the house to keep several guns where we could get to them if needed. My eyes searched the room, and I knew we were fucked. By the time that Major got out of the shower, he would come downstairs to our lifeless bodies.

"What do you want?" Crimson asked. Her voice didn't hold a hint of fear, but her hands that stayed on me were shaking bad.

"What the fuck do you mean what do I want? You should know after all this time. At first, I wanted Keyionte', but after she pulled that shit a couple of weeks ago, all I want is you two bitches' dead. Maybe things can get back to the way it was before you two bitches entered our lives. I can even find it in myself to forgive Major for tapping into my pussy." He gave us a lopsided smirk as he kept his gun aimed at us.

"After all the shit you have done, do you really think all is just supposed to be forgiven like that? You think Quinton and Major will choose your life over there's?" I quizzed.

"Haven't you heard I'm crazy as hell. They know that the voices in my head tell me to do all types of shit. Plus, if they can forgive me for killing Tan, they can forgive me for all that shit and killing you hoes too. They want to put me in a home, so I'll do a couple of years there, and then I can come home and put this entire crazy act to rest," he said smugly before cocking his gun like he was tired of talking to us.

I was disgusted. The entire time this motherfucker was only pretending like he was crazy. He had been beating my ass and putting all of our lives in danger for what?

"What was the fucking point of all this?" I waved my hands around. I was a ball of flames on the inside. I had never in my life wanted a body on my conscience, but at this moment and time, I wanted his.

"The point of all of this is to become the 'God' that streets deserve. Quinton is too soft to run this shit. He laid eyes on this bitch and acted like he had never gotten pussy a day in his life, and let's not talk about Major. He has always been a second-hand type of nigga. He's second to Quinton, and evidently, he loves my sloppy seconds. Let's make a deal. I'll try to forgive you for all this and let you live if you stay with me and promise not to run away. I'll just kill this bitch, and we can take over all this once I'm out of the nut house."

I balled my fist up at my sides. I could smell the copper of his blood hitting the air from my hands.

"How about you fuck yourself on the way to hell."

At that time, I heard three shots go off in the room before I felt a burning sensation go through my shoulder. I heard bodies dropping around me. Crimson's father Joel and Quinton were yelling her name, and Major was yelling my name. Everything went in slow motion as I turned and saw Crimson and her father on the floor. Quinton was sliding across the floor at her side as she yelled for her dad before her eyes closed. I dropped down to my knees trying to make it to her right before Major sat behind me wrapping his arms around me.

"NO, CRIMSON! NO, DON'T LEAVE ME!"

I was crying so hard that my body vibrated as I continued to try to get to her. My heart was hurting so bad that I forgot about my own pain until Major pressed his shirt to my wound. I walked over to Rush's dead body. He had a gunshot wound in the front of his head and one going through his chest. I stared at his body for a minute before I started kicking him over and over. Major let me go for it until I screamed out and started crying. I was a broken woman.

Epilogue

QUINTON

Major and I each had one of her hands in ours as we stood in the graveyard waiting for her to say her peace.

"I know we didn't get the chance to say our peace before your untimely demise, but I want you to know that I'm sorry for everything I've said to you. I know none of this would have happened if it wasn't for me, and you don't know how much I wish that I could take back. I'm not saying that I regret meeting the love of my life, but I do regret losing my best friend."

We stood there silently waiting for the thickness of her emotions to pass. Her words had my heart breaking.

"I have so many memories of us that I could share, but I don't know if I would be able to make it through telling them. I just want you to know that I understand where you were coming from, and I know that this is the price I have to pay for loving a street god. I love you, daddy."

Crimson wiped the tears from her eyes, put her fingers to her lips, and placed them on her father's headstone. He had come to Major's house to make things right with Crimson the day he was killed. The bullet that was meant to kill Keyionte' had gone through three people. It had hit Keyionte' in the shoulder, Crimson in the chest missing her heart by half an inch, but killed her father going in his stomach, ripping through his intestines. My heart went out to Crimson, and I felt responsible for her father's death because I had given him the address to make things right with her. Rush died instantly, and we couldn't tell which bullet killed him because Major hit him in the heart, and I got him in the head. To find out that everything he had done was an act let me know that he had been jealous since we were kids. I was willing to give Rush everything my brother Tan had worked so hard for only to find out that he was the nigga that had him killed. It's a fucked up feeling to have your day one cross you and to have to put him to rest, but that's the price you have to pay being a nigga like myself.

"You ready for this vacation?" Keyionte' asked Crimson as we walked back towards our cars.

"I hope y'all are ready, but we have to finish shopping," Jinx interrupted as she grabbed Crimson's hand pulling her and Keyionte' to her truck.

Crimson

"You never leave loose ends," Blaze told us as we pulled up to a mansion not too far from their house. Today had been exhausting. We went to the funeral, then shopping, and now this.

"I don't think I can do this," I told them seriously, I wasn't ready for all this, not to mention I didn't think that I could make it over the gate we were looking at.

"Don't turn pussy on me now. Think about that fact that you won't see your father anymore, and he is the reason why we have to finish this now. If the men won't do it, we have to," Jinx told me seriously.

I took a deep breath and made my way over the fence. It had a big F on the front of it for Ferrari. We stayed in the shadows like Blaze and Jinx had taught us. We went to the back door that we knew would be open. Jinx and Blaze had cased this house since we left their house weeks ago. We walked through the dark living room.

"I told you they were coming here." Rio laughed then four flashlights pointed at us.

"Fuck y'all," Jinx let out before turning making her way to the back door. We all followed her.

"I swear we don't have any fun anymore," Blaze said as we walked out to our cars.

"Meet us at the airport!" one of them yelled out, but as I got ready to get in the car, I felt Quinton snake his arms around me.

"What's up, babe?" I asked him.

"I don't want you into this shit, you hear me?" he said, turning me around to him. His words were so sincere. What he didn't know was that I made myself a promise when I met my dad in that haze of blinding light when I got shot. I would never be caught slipping again.

"This is your price of making me fall for a street god."

I kissed his lips and got in the car with my girls. Quinton had changed my life in so many ways, some good and some bad, but I will forever live my life being Enticed by a Street God.

The End

CPSIA information can be obtained
at www.ICGtesting.com
Printed in the USA
LVHW051516270619
622553LV00002B/263/P

9 781071 063767